BALLS

A Tale of Radical Feminism and a Girl

SIMON PLASTER

mossikpress@mail.com

Library of Congress Cataloguing-in-Publication Data

Plaster, Simon [5.24.2015]

Balls: A Tale of Radical Feminism and a Girl
by Simon Plaster

p. cm

ISBN 978-0-991-44804-3

1. Humor—Fiction.

2. Oklahoma, United States—Fiction.

3. Feminism—Fiction.

4. College Sports—Fiction.

I. Title

10 9 8 7 6 5 4 3 2 1

Manufactured in the United States of AmericaFirst Edition

SP/MP

BALLS

A Tale of Radical Feminism and a Girl

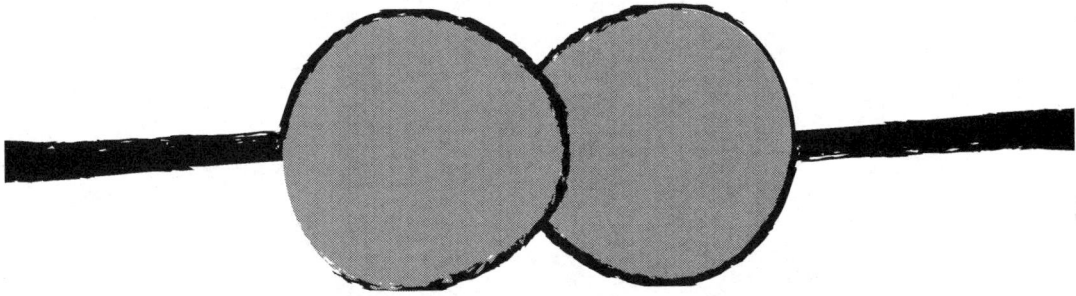

SIMON PLASTER

FOREWARD

TITLE IX

No person in the United States shall, on the basis of gender, be excluded from participation in, be denied the benefits of, or be subjected to discrimination under any educational program or activity receiving federal assistance.

OFFICE OF LIEUTENANT GOVERNOR
STATE OF OKLAHOMA

The Honorable Pricilla "Prissy" O'Fallon
<u>For Immediate Release</u>

By executive proclamation, Lieutenant Governor Pricilla "Prissy" O'Fallon today announced that the Oklahoma State Prison for the criminally young ("OSP") has been re-named and shall hereafter be known as the Oklahoma Institute of Correctology ("OIC"). "This action is in keeping with OIC's ongoing development as an ivory tower of higher rehabilitation," said the Lieutenant Governor, before smashing a bottle of champagne against one of the rusted iron gates of the prison. In her address to penal dignitaries and invited guests from outside the walls of its McAlester, OK campus, Ms. O'Fallon noted that OIC has already supplanted the University of Oklahoma as a football powerhouse, earning for the Sooner State millions of dollars in TV revenue. "And with upcoming admission of young female inmates to OIC, Title IX provisions requiring sexual sameness will no longer block us from federal funding," she said. "Even more eyes of the nation will be upon us in the months and years ahead, not on, say, the Massachusetts Institute of <u>Tech</u>nology, that specializes in teaching unsocial science and does not even have a popular football team. So the updated name is necessary and desirable to convey accurate and positive understanding of what the Oklahoma State Corrections Department motto is all about."

Namely, *sine disciplinum, omnia manent inirium*, or in other words, "without correction, everything stays wrong." To the end of putting an end to wrong - doing by persons under twenty-five years of age, engagement of a head warden, to be known as "Dean of Correctees," will be announced within days. "The Dean will be unequivocally in charge," Ms. O'Fallon unequivocally stated. "High standards of correctology will not be compromised by, say, over-emphasis on football or other extracurricular activities as has been the unfortunate case at certain other correctional institutions that shall remain nameless." She was of course discreetly referring to the bankruptcy of most of the nation's public universities resulting from collapse of bigtime college football and misdirected focus on discredited academic ologies.

"I repeat," the Lieutenant Governor repeated, before smashing an empty second bottle against the prison gate, "OIC shall be a prairie 'Harvard of Correctology', where rehabilitation of our sons <u>and</u> daughters by means of strict application of modern principles of attitude and behavior correction will lead us onward into a brave new world."

FOR MORE INFORMATION:
Contact media@ofallonforgovernor.org.

ONE

Henryetta—correctly spelled with a y, just like the name of the little ol' Oklahoma town that still held her prisoner—looked up from her desk in the storefront office of the *Weekly Herald*, and sighed. A framed page from *The New York Times* hung on a wall across from her. **SHE DID IT!** headlined an article above a stock photo of a cow standing in a pasture, and a byline told that she her own self, *Henryetta P. Hebert, Special Correspondent*, had wrote the piece about global warming a/k/a climate change. Her boss, Mr. Harold Mixon, had put the souvenir together for her and said it was like the first dollar bill he'd earned as a paperboy that was framed on a wall across from his desk. There would be plenty more big city newspaper bylines to follow, he'd said, proud as the breeder of a blue-ribbon piglet at the Okmulgee County Fair. But so far, not *The New York Times* nor anyone else had offered her a real job that would get her headed toward winning one of those Pulitzer Prizes that she'd hankered for since becoming a reporter for her high school newspaper, *The Monthly Egg*.

Henryetta resisted an urge to take down the framed article,

and with another sigh, returned to opening the day's mail. "Huh," awhile ago, Leon Corn, a high school classmate, had listed her as a "character reference," which was odd as socks on a rooster. Back when she was a cheerleader, he was one of the hogs who played in the line of the football team, though he usually got kicked out of games before halftime for stomping on someone's head or poking another player in the eye. Since then he had got to be bigger, and even uglier, with a crooked scar running from his forehead down his nose, to where a ratty red beard finished off his unbecoming face appearance. The two of them had tangled in tenth grade, a time or two since, and she still made a point to cuss him ever' time they happened to cross paths. Why the sumbitch would have wanted her to put checkmarks in the boxes of a "Letter of Recommendation" was a mystery. And now he had sent her a *Hallmark* thank you card, sayin'…Ding! Her computer signaled receipt of e-mail:

To: H.E. Hebert…From: G.G. Carpenter…Re: Employment Opportunity for Bylined News Correspondent…Reply ASAP to Femichismo!

Henryetta clicked a link, which took her to a page headed *About Us.* She read that *Femichismo!* was a site dedicated to both aggregation of published news articles and firsthand reporting about specific events and general developments of particular importance to modern women. A masthead indicated that G.G. Carpenter, Editor-in-Chief, had previously worked for *Newsweek* and the *The Daily Beast.* Listed correspondents also had impressive credentials, including boasts of bylines in big city newspapers and famous magazines. Excited as all get out, Henryetta went to the news site's home page:

BALLS! SAID THE QUEEN

A color photo showed Hillary Clinton, looking well fed in a bright red dress, smiling with bright red lips and lots of teeth. Beside her stood her husband, Bill, white-haired, thin as a fiddle string, feeble in appearance and glum as an old gelding waiting to be picked up by a glue factory wagon. A sub-head referred to them as **America's Queen Victoria and Consort In a Can.** The news copy…*Like Britain's legendary self-empowered queen, model for Lewis Carroll's equally renown Queen of Hearts who used hedgehogs for croquet balls in Wonderland, Hillary has vowed to play with Rush Limbaugh's fuzzy testicles on the White House lawn after the next election. "Off with their heads!" she also proclaimed, in response to extreme right-wing opponents of a constitutional amendment creating a legal presumption of criminal male guilt in college campus hetero-rape cases. She was of course referring to the "heads" of erect penises of jocks and frat boys. So when pundits refer to Hillary as our Victorian Queen of Hearts in Wonderland, and to her putting her "Prince Albert" in a can, what they mean is that gender justice is coming soon.*

Bohica!

Henryetta read a few more lines without noticing any news of particular importance to her own self; but then did note that two or three small ads along the right-hand side of the home page seemed to be for sex toys, including one for a battery-powered "Bean Flicker" endorsed by Hillary Clinton. Of an altogether different sort, another ad saying just *JOIN TODAY!* might have been for Senior Campfire Girls or some women's group like that, Henryetta reckoned. The troop's logo was a sort of Native American design: Two rosy pink circles mounted on a horizontal stick, lined up above small pink pyramids that could have stood for either distant mountains or maybe campfire flames. Shucks, a job with *Femichismo!* wouldn't half measure up to one at *The*

New York Times, maybe not even to the employment she already had at the *Weekly Herald,* but…After not finding any other offers in the pile of paper mail, Henryetta returned to the *Femichismo!* website and began to type:

To: G.G. Carpenter…From: Henryetta Hebert…Re: Employment Opportunity for Bylined News Correspondent…

Dear Mr. or Ms. Carpenter…How much would the job pay, and more important, where would I have to relocate to? See, Henryetta OK is the hometown that my mother, Wynona Sue, named me for. I've been what you might call stuck to here for my whole life. And I'm already past twenty!

Henryetta sent the e-mail and went back to puzzling over the card from Leon Corn, while also wondering what could be keeping her boss, Mr. Harold Mixon. Ordinarily, he would have come through the door by now in his odd way of walking. As an unusually thoughtful boy in his youthful years, Mr. Harold had decided, according to his own self, that for man or boy to swing his arms when walking was to swagger. So he had trained his self to keep his arms straight when he walked, in a sort of moving at-attention posture, that seemed to have transferred swagger to an up-and-down bob. He was generally thought of locally as a character — specifically a character called "The Great Stinker" — due to the fact that above his editorials, **From Where I Sit,** the paper always ran a picture of a famous statue of a naked man setting on what could have been a toilet, with his chin resting on a hand that was propped on a knee.

But Mr Harold was smart as a school teacher about most things. In the 1960s he went to college at Princeton, back east in New Jersey. And there he not only played on the freshman basketball team, as a member of the University Press Club he also worked as a stringer for big city newspapers. Now he was getting up in years, of course; the hair on his head was getting thin, but he still…Henryetta's eye-phone buzzed.

"Call me G.G." said a woman's voice. "I'll call you Henry or Etta or H.E. In answer to your questions, pay for all correspondents is based on lineage published, which works out to about thirty to forty cents cents per word. Hence our motto: 'Brevity is the soul of pith'. And here's the best part about being one of our bylined correspondents: Though I and a small staff are based in Boulder, there will be no need for you to relocate. Welcome to *Femichismo!* H.E."

"Boulder, Colorado?" said Henryetta. "I wouldn't mind movin' up there, but at a rate of thirty or forty cents a word…"

"No need, H.E. All our correspondents are in the field where the action is. Indeed, it was for the very purpose of getting coverage in your, er, overlooked region, that led us to you. Assuming you have a reliable car for getting around, you can happily continue to carry on from that hometown you are so attached to. And keep your other job at …"

"I drive an old yellow Checker cab for a car. It's odometer is on its third or fourth go 'round, it's in need of a new set of used tires, and…"

"'Yellow Checker', how perfect for an investigative journalist. I wonder if I could find one up here in the Rocky…Uh oh, gotta go, H.E. One of our other 'yellow checkers' is reporting in from the Holy Land. She's on vacation, but working on a Christmas Special: GOD UP ON RAPE RAP! Poor Mary, bound in wedlock but—good for her—still a proud virgin. Talk about a powerful male taking advantage of His position of authority. Talk about patriarchy! That's the kind of slant on news we're looking for, H.E. Get to it." Click.

Minutes after she hung up, Henryetta got an e mail from *Femichismo!* A one-page contract in real small print said the online news publication company would not be responsible for content of pieces sent in by correspondents, nor liable for any incorrect statements or libelous accusations that got printed. A correspondent was an "independent contractor," free and in fact encouraged to hold down other full time jobs for obtaining firsthand information, in addition to checking for reports from local news sources twenty-four hours a day. Henryetta went to thinking the "position" she'd been offered was all broth and no beans—about like Mr. Harold over-modestly described the honor of being a Princeton University Press Club stringer— and at that very same moment, her boss called-in to the office.

"Henryetta, you'll never guess who's comin' to town," he said, panting like a fat dog on a hot day; and he was right about that; she couldn't imagine whose arrival could have got Mr. Harold so lathered up. "Shat!" he hollered, "Shatner Lapp! His bus from Tulsa is due to deliver him to Okmulgee within the hour. I should be back to town with him before noon."

Shatner Lapp! That <u>was</u> exciting news. "Shat" was Mr. Harold's hero, and rightly so, from back when they were in college, and in the Princeton Press Club together. She'd seen a picture of the "whiz kid" in an old yearbook: Tall, thin, long straight hair swept back, a scarf around his neck, the very image of a dashing news reporter. And from Mr. Harold, she'd heard all about Shatner Lapp's career in journalism: In college, as just a press club stringer, he'd got a story in his Pennsylvania hometown paper about Shriners being in Memphis, Tennessee for a convention only a week before Dr. Martin Luther King Jr. got shot there, which led to an F.B.I. investigation. He was a war correspondent, who covered the anti-Vietnam War protests in San Francisco. "And Shat was first to report that Mohammed Ali was gay," she recalled Mr. Harold telling, "which turned out to be technically right, according to usage of the term by some back then."

Most important to Henryetta, Mr. Harold had wrote to his old friend in recent years about her, asking if he could pull on some strings to get her on the payroll of a big city newspaper. Unfortunately, the famous roving correspondent seemed to always be roving in some far-off place, unable to help or even to answer Mr. Harold's letters. But now, by golly…Henryetta jumped up out of her chair and hurried to a bathroom off a rear hallway. Back with paper towels and a bottle of *Windex*, she shined up the glass in the frame holding the *Times* piece headlined **SHE DID IT!** After straightening its position, she moved a chair against the wall directly under the frame, then stepped back.

Yep, anyone walking into the office, such as, say, Mr. Shatner Lapp, would bump right into *The New York Times* article by *Henryetta P. Hebert, Special Correspondent.*

TWO

At the wheel of her 1995 Suburu Outback, accompanied by Martha Washington in the seat beside her, Ester Frigg—yes, Frigg—neared the terminus of her southbound career path from Harvard to the Oklahoma Institute of Correctology. Though her unfortunate name had provoked brutal sexual assaults by moronic males since her teens, Ester was determined to not give her verbal rapists the satisfaction of forcing her to change it. She had always been thicker-skinned than, say, her former colleague, the radical feminist, Connie Dickperson *nee* Connie Dickman. Only after turning fifty a year ago had she begun to become what some called…"Is it 'over sensitive' to be traumatized by the name of this highway?" she rhetorically asked Martha Washington, a Persian cat. The fact that she was required to travel to her new position via a despicably named "Indian Nation," not "Indigenous Peoples Nation" Turnpike, was doubly hurtful, given the circumstances of her departure from Harvard.

Ester sighed. But for a single misstep, by next year or the next she might have finally achieved tenure at the prestigious

Ivy League university. As a full professor in its Correctology Deparment, free from the hassle and harm of petty internal political machinations, she would have continued to shape the minds of younger generations by comfortably thinking great thoughts, writing and teaching. Her published doctoral dissertation—*Eye for an Eye: A Shortsighted Concept of Visually Less-Abled Justice*—had led to countless other scholarly papers in which she had expanded upon her thesis, to-wit: Just as the death penalty was demonstrably ineffective in deterring murder, so too were all conventional means of punishment for all anti-social acts unacceptably and unnecessarily cruel and unusual. A comprehensive book, already well received in draft form, would soon bring to prominence her fully developed Frigg Theory, to-wit: In keeping with Amish ways, shunning of social miscreants was far more effective than incarceration for deterring unacceptable behavior. It had worked in practice, at Harvard, where she had shunned a fellow Assistant Professor for his untoward wise cracking that bordered on sexual harassment.

Ester reached across to give Martha Washington a reassuring pat, and again sighed. She had never heard of the Oklahoma Institute of Correctology until being offered its Deanship, and still knew not much about the small college except that not until the coming fall semester—"Believe it or not, Martha"—was "OIC" to admit women! Though previously not widely recognized for her efforts as an activist for sexual justice—a caption below a large photo on the front page of the *Boston Globe* had not identified her by name, only as a protester—the Oklahoma Lieutenant Governor, a woman named O'Fallon, must have seen it; and must have been favorably impressed by the content of the placard she carried that matched the demand she was shown shouting: STOP CAMPUS RAPE EPIDEMIC! Concerned that the epidemic could spread to the "home of indigenous people," Ms. O'Fallon had offered total authority to oversee OIC during its transformation into an enlightened co-educational institute of higher attitude adjustment and behavioral correction. Ester had been not particularly interested, only flattered, but... An insensitive high school sports team bumper sticker on the vehicle in front of her — GO REDSKINS! — triggered a painful recollection:

"Thinking of moving out to the 'home of the red man', are we?" the same fellow Assistant Professor had sneered, in obviously jealous reaction to her announcement of the OIC offer. So of course she had reported his utterance of the racial slur of indigenous peoples to Harvard's Administrative Board. But..."Aha!" the Ad Board's Chief Inquisitor had shouted. "The term 'Oklahoma' is itself a despicable, though also an indigenous slur that literally translates to 'home of the red man'. You spoke the offensive word yourself, ex-Assistant Professor Frigg!" he thundered. "And have added insult to injury by boasting of your pending association with an institution bearing the very name that singles out people of Native American misfortune, thereby drawing hurtful attention to their marginalized status in the corrupt white man's society in which they are forced to live. The letters O-K-L-A-H-O-M-A have no place within these ivy-covered walls, and neither do you. Frigg off, Frigg! Harvard hereby shuns you in the First Degree!"

And now, third, fourth, fifth sixth and seventh triggers of other trauma appeared in Ester's rearview mirror. "Turn away and close your eyes," she said to Martha Washington, who was no doubt still in deep psychological pain from a recent loss of fur to a randy tomcat. As the barbarous gang of motorcyclists came alongside her Suburu, one of them yelled in her direction: "I'd druther you not!" How offensive and hurtful! No doubt he was referring to one of the many slogans plastered on her vehicle; perhaps the one urging others to VOTE FOR NADER, or the one: KEEP GOD OUT OF THE BEDROOM, or the one: CUT OFF MY REPRO RIGHTS/ I'LL CUT OFF YOURS, or perhaps the one from that women's empowerment conference in Maine: MACHO MEN: SHUCK 'EM! But no, more likely the leather-clad brute had shown such rude disrespect for the many slogans expressing protest against cruel exploitation of animal companions: I WEAR MY OWN SKIN, or possibly: I WOULD RATHER GO NAKED.

Could the gang of hoodlums—with *Big-Balled Bulls* emblazoned in pink on their black jackets—possibly be odious frat boys akin to big-balled members of Harvard's notorious men-only A.D. Club; and be also en route to OIC? If so, "you have my permission, indeed I encourage you to scratch their oversized pink testicles, should the opportunity arise," Ester said to Martha Washington; who purred, no doubt with relish at the prospect of sweet revenge for the sexual assault she had suffered at the claws of the latest "Tom, Dick or Harry" to cross her path.

Ester reached across to stroke the long, mixed-brownish fur of her beloved animal companion, and "sister." They were much alike, people said, and it was true: Both Martha Washington and she had sweet, gentle personalities. Both of them were most at home in an atmosphere of security and serenity, but were adaptable. Martha Washington had all the Persian traits most esteemed by the Cat Fanciers Association: Large expressive eyes. Short, heavy-boned legs to support her stout body, and keep her feet firmly on the ground. Yes, they were very much like sisters, Ester was pleased to say to herself. Though it was also true that while she usually wore her long Martha-colored hair in a bun, without benefit of having trapped a an up-and-coming husband she was often compared favorably to the younger Hillary Clinton—also a Wellesley girl—who only in her post-graduate years affected the blue contact lenses and light hair of a mixed-Siamese breed.

Minutes after the rude verbal and visual assault on both Martha Washington and her by the motorcycle jock, Ester took the "McAlester" exit from the turnpike and drove toward the northwest edge of the small town. Skimpy materials provided to her described the OIC campus as walled and gated, also as having a "yard" like Harvard's original setting. Ah, she now saw from a distance its impressive facade. As she drove on, the institute's surrounding whitewashed walls loomed higher and higher. Passing under an arched metal sign…"Uh oh, Martha." High chain-link fences topped with razor wire seemed to indicate presence of a bad neighborhood nearby. With women soon to be enrolled, Ester welcomed the protective measures to keep undesirable elements at bay. After driving farther down a charming tree-lined lane, she parked her brown vehicle in front of a stately two-story structure across from the walled and gated campus. A small wood sign on a post quaintly identified the official Dean's residence by the British old school term, "Warden's House."

Ester's, and no doubt Martha Washington's delight in their new surroundings was then dampened, however, first by the smell of fried bacon in the air, then by the appearance and disrespectful slouch of a sallow-faced man in a campus security force uniform, blocking the doorway into <u>her</u> house. He introduced himself as Goober Somebody, "the man in charge of men." How dare he!

"I'll take care of the men inside the walls," he said, while moving a toothpick from one side of his mouth to the other.

"Soon as those split-tails get bussed in, you can coddle them over in the old F Unit, and do your paperwork here in your cozy house office, where it's safe; though I can't promise that cat there will survive past sundown, on account of my dogs."

"You, sir, and your dogs shall be the ones to not survive the day if so much as a single fang is laid on my animal companion, Martha Washington," said Ester. "As Dean, I am in total charge of OIC. I myself shall 'handle' male correctees, and the young women, who shall not be referred to as 'split-tails' nor by any other feather of demeaning bird mascot. Understood?!"

Mr. Goober Somebody slouched lower and dug his hands deeper into the trouser pockets of his uniform.

"Co-ed status shall be established campus-wide," Ester continued; "not only in class rooms and cafeterias, but in the residential dorms also. In case you failed to notice, my dear sir, this is the twenty-first century!"

"I'll leave you with my resignation and these," he said, handing over his badge and a ring of keys, "along with the official OIC welcoming word for newcomers: Bohica!"

"Bohica" was no doubt an indigenous peoples' term, she imagined, as Martha Washington scampered through a doorway into another room. Ester followed. Ah, a large office greeted her; furnished with two ordinary desks, but behind one of them, at last: The Big Chair, befitting a woman of her more than ample ability to fill it.

THREE

The man who walked into the *Weekly Herald* office alongside Mr. Harold…Henryetta only semi-recognized the college yearbook "whiz kid" as the now famous journalist, Shatner Lapp: Still tall, though semi-stooped. Thinner, if anything; in fact, downright scrawny in the neck where a scarf would have been useful to cover up a frayed and over-sized shirt collar. Nor was his hair likely long, straight and blonde no more, she reckoned, 'cause he had on his head a frizzy, jet black wig. Looking around the office with outstretched arms, "Ah, the smell of printers ink, the roar of the presses!" he said. "Schweet! God, I've missed the feeling of an oldtime news room, Harry. Where do you stash the grease that keeps the presses humming?" Looking shamed as a puppy dog, caught doing his business on a living room carpet, Mr. Harold admitted that he kept no Who-Struck-John on the premises; then brightened up to announce that the P's-and-Q's pool hall and quaint cafe would start serving spiritous beverages at noon. "Shat" looked at his watch, then stumbled past the chair set under the framed *New York Times* piece, with nary a glance at its headline—**SHE DID IT!**—nor at its bylined writer,

Henryetta P. Hebert, Special Correspondent, settin' across from what she did like a strawberry-blonde pointer dog staring at a tree knot.

"So this is the so-called 'spelled-with-an-a-*Weakly*...*Harold*, also spelled-with-an-a'," said Mr. Harold's old friend, with a chuckle. "Oh yeah, Harry, I've kept my nose in the air through the years. 'Good news and good deals for the good people of, uh, this county,' that's your motto, right? Cubie D and I had a good laugh over the motto, along with a few drinks at the Bombay Press Club awhile back. You remember Cubie, gone all yogi now, but whatta guy he used to be, right, Harry?"

Mr. Harold a/k/a "Harry" cleared his throat. "This here is, well, you might say my 'protege' of sorts, Miss Henryetta Hebert," he said, blushing like he was embarrassed to be boastful about hisself. "And on the wall there, that's a piece she wrote for *The New York Times*."

Mr. Lapp moved toward the framed article, squinted at it for about two seconds, then turned to her. "Yeah, I saw this," he said; "typical *Times* dirty trick. But don't let the bastards make you cry, Honey. Keep the page right here, front and center, as a lesson learned the hard way. Right, Harry?"

Dirty trick? Lesson? Probably in answer to her mouth semi-gaping open, and Mr. Harold's too, the veteran newspaper man went on to explain: The *Times* had put her byline on the piece as "special correspondent" to distance itself from, and discredit its content, he said. By framing doubt about the official left wing line on climate change and its cause as a report from "Hicksville,"*Times* editors had reinforced the exact opposite view, while at the same time providing its "flock of eastern elitist sheep" with a good laugh. According to Shatner Lapp, since publishing the article to "mock" new scientific findings from Oklahoma, and news reporting by her, *The New York Times* had continued to pimp anti-coal, anti-capitalist, anti-American alternative energies, such as windmills, with its ongoing "end of the world" morality tale. "Sort of a new version of the Jesus story," he said. "Scare the bejesus out of the sheep, then promise salvation to true believers in statism and worldwide redistribution of American wealth.

"Mares and goats may eat oats down here in Oklahoma, Honey," he said, picking up the current *Weekly Herald* off Henryetta's desk, "but if you ever want to get off the 'farm' and on the staff of a big city newspaper, you're gonna have to pick your stories from the all-organic garden sprouting Ivy League fruits and produce; then cook 'em according to the right recipe. Get it?"

Henryetta didn't get it, but tried to not let on for fear of looking like a bumpkin from "Hicksville."

"Take this little item, for instance," the experienced journalism expert then said, after a quick scan of the newspaper she and Mr. Harold had put out a few days before. "There's not any mention of the hit-and-run victim being African-American, and by editorializing that the outbreak of racial conflict was an 'accident', you buried the larger truth that this bigoted old woman is like thousands of others in this community who..."

"Hit-and-run? Ms. Vickers didn't even notice she had bumped into that old man's shopping cart in the Farmer Billsmart parking lot. And the police blotter didn't say nothin' about him bein' African-American. His sack of tomatoes was the only 'victim' and..."

"Who's to say he <u>wasn't</u> African-American," said Mr. Lapp. "And 'Cops Refuse to File Charges Against Reckless White Driver' would have been a better sub-head than 'No One Hurt

Except Tomatoes.' Chances are the victim is blind, possibly as a result of prior racial attack or...Look, uh, Marietta, *The New York Times* motto, for instance—'All The News Fit To Print'—means that one way or another news has to be made to fit the ideological templates welded to its presses. Same for the other big city rags. There are only a few stories that click. 'Racial Bias and Oppression of African-Americans' is the peoples' favorite; it never gets old.

"A reporter's job is to re-tell it over and over, with different slants that hone the ageless mythic narrative," he continued, while peeking at his big fake Rolex like it was a time clock ticking down minutes to end of his work shift. "Yeah, you've got to tell the tale over and over, sort of like our patron saints of journalism—Mathew, Mark and, uh, the other one—did with the first edition of the Jesus story, that got picked-up and put in book form. As a matter of fact, Harry," he said, swiveling his head to Mr. Harold, "the reason I came down here is that I've got a fresh angle for a *Weekly Herald* series."

Henryetta argued, or tried to argue, that the known facts of her little ol' story likely didn't have no "racial angle" to be told about; that in the little ol' town of Henryetta, Oklahoma there were not as many as a hundred African-Americans; that relations among them and about fifty-five hundred white and Native American townfolk had never had any noticeable "bias" or "oppression" that anybody knew of. But Mr. Lapp's mind seemed to have moved back to other interests. "Say, Harry," he said, studying his watch again, and ignoring her, "that pool hall you mentioned oughta be starting to rack 'em up about now. Let's hotfoot over there and beat the rush."

Mr. Harold invited her to come along, and Henryetta, anxious to make a better impression on the great man, Shatner

Lapp—including a correcter impression of her name, Henryetta-spelled-with-a-y—decided she'd better change her tune. "I'll check the facts of that hit-and-run with Police Chief Potter," she said, as they hurried out the door. "I'll give Ms. Vickers a grillin' and look up that possibly black and blind man she ran into. I'll do a re-write and…"

"Fishwrap," her journalism criticizer replied. "Find another story of blatant racism in town. They're bound to be common as pig tracks, in need of nothing more than a fresh slant."

About a block down the Main Street sidewalk, passing by The Best Little Hair House in Town—employment place of Henryetta's own mother, Wynona Sue—their important visitor stopped in his tracks. "Uh, have you got a C-note on you, Harry?" he said, patting the chest pockets of his semi-ratty old sport coat. "I need to pick up something here at this beauty shop, and seem to have left my wallet with my luggage in the trunk of your car." Henryetta volunteered to run back and get it, but Mr. Harold's old friend held her back. "I'll only be a minute," he said, as Mr. Harold counted out some twenty-dollar bills into his outstretched palm. "We don't wanna miss the day's first pour, right, Harry?"

Henryetta was glad to wait outside, if only to avoid embarrassment of seeing her mother, Wynona Sue, meet up with Shatner Lapp. Pickins of men had been slim to none recently for Wynona Sue, and for the other gals who gave and got beauty treatments in the hair house too. They were sure to get after the stranger from out of town like a brood of Rhode Island Red, or blonde, hens on a roly-poly. Probably for approximately the same reason, Mr. Harold also waited on the sidewalk for his friend to pick-up something. "Shat's always been what you might call a colorful character," he said. "He's always had a one-of-a-kind nose for human interest news angles and an original way with words. Back in our college press club days, he used to say that being a news reporter was like being a bartender: Sure, three dashes of bitters might dilute the alcoholic content of an Old Fashioned cocktail, but six dashes—maybe two cubes of sugar and an extra cup o' fizz—will improve the mix and make the whole jar more palatable. No good barkeep would serve up straight grain alcohol, meaning just plain facts. There's a lot for both of us to learn by just listening to Shat shoot the…breeze."

Then, out of the beauty parlor came the colorful character in a semi-huff, to judge by his stride. "Well, there you go, Honey," he said to Henryetta, "racial bigotry right under your nose. That little whore house might as well have a sign on the door sayin' 'Colored Not Allowed'. They don't even…"

"It's a hair house, not a whore house!" Henryetta protested. "My own mother, Wynona Sue, works there and would never…"

"Whatever," he replied, with a wave of his hand, like flies were swarmin' around him or somethin'. "All I know is that I could have got a slice of snapper in there and walked out with ninety bucks still in my pocket. But they don't serve, at any price, a jar of *Bronzer or Midnight Magic* or *Colortration*, not even *Miss Jessie's Curly Meringue* for fizz control or any other product for African-American hair and skin. No doubt N-words fill the air in there like fleas."

"Wynona Sue has never been known to take cash from a gentleman friend 'til a second or third date!"

Having made such a bad family impression, by the time they got to the P's-and-Q's, Henryetta reckoned any chances of Mr. Shatner Lapp helping her get a big city newspaper job were thin as thirsty cattle. He ignored her after they set down at a table, and paid no attention to Mr. Harold's heavy-handed hints about her career ambitions, obviously being more interested in ordering a jar of Who-Struck-John and studying the cafe's menu blackboard. "Oysters, how quaint," he said. "I didn't know they served such fare out here on the plain."

"Oh yes," she said, "we're really quite urbane," and that got his attention. Mr. Lapp looked at her, surprised maybe that she had recognized—and maybe interrupted—his spiel of a fairly not well known piece of cowboy poetry about a confused gal from back east ordering up a dozen Rocky Mountain oysters to eat raw. Or maybe he was surprised that for some other reason a red-dirt girl like her might once upon a time have looked up the word "urbane."

"Call me Shat," he said, "I'll call you Jenetta." Then, after he'd been served and gulped down about half a "jar" of Who-Struck-John—without mixin' in any bitters or fizz—"Ah, hair of the dog," he said, before going on to lecture her in a gentler tone: "See, Honey, journalism is all about weaving a narrative," he said, "and every narrative, hell, every joke for that matter, should have a moral. A news story, if told right, is a morality tale of right and wrong, good and evil, black and white. But to find the moral of any news, a reporter has to look past the obvious facts into the dirt and grime between the cracks, where truths are hidden like roaches."

As Mr. Shat paused to finish off his beverage, and wave for another jar, Henryetta began to understand why he, as opposed to say, his college classmate, Mr. Harold, had made such a name for hisself in her chosen profession. She yearned for an opportunity to tell a morality tale. If only..."Take that little whore house down the street," her new journalism instructor said. "Honey, go in there and grill those so-called beauticians. I guarantee: Roaches will scurry out of hairy little cracks by the dozen, right, Harry?"

FOUR

Though not yet noon, Leon Corn was out of bed, unshowered but fully dressed in just overalls, no shirt, and well-worn, shit-kickin' cowboy boots; ready for the big day ahead of him. With remains from a quart-size can of beer left over from the night before, or the night before that one, he washed down a biscuit-size tablet of *Stud* testosterone booster for horses and looked around the bedroom of the permanently-located mobile home where he had misspent almost his whole life. His daddy had unhitched the pull-truck and took off the day he himself started kindergarten, leaving his mother and him broke-down there for the past fifteen or sixteen years. An old treadless tire leaning against a wall took Leon down a memory lane: It was the first one he ever stole. Because he'd slashed it before jacking up his mama's van, the pawn shop had turned it down flat; but there was still sentimental value to the souvenir. The wall itself was plastered with magazine center-spreads of naked females, all with copies of the same slightly freckled face from a high school yearbook stuck on them. He'd had a crush on that strawberry-blonde girl, Henryetta, since childhood.

Leon sighed, pushed open a window and relieved himself onto a weedy driveway outside. He looked into a mirror and ran his fingers through the red whiskers on his face. He wanted to look his best today, in case Henryetta came by later to cry on his bare shoulder—the one where he had tattooed her name inside a yellow heart next to an also yellow rose with a spider on it—not the other one where his friend, Gary, had blotted out *Mama* and put his own name inside a matching yellow heart. Misting up at the thought of leaving Henryetta, his happy home, and unhappy life behind him, Leon climbed out the window—as he had done so many times before—and crossed the weedy, semi-graveled driveway to the window of Gary Durland's bedroom. Like he had done so many of the same many times before, he climbed through Gary's window. No doubt dreading his send-off, the old gang was already gathered: Drinking beer and smoking weed; all except Sherry What's-Her-Name, the fraternity sweetheart, who was straddling Gary's parked motorcycle, with her nose stuck in the gas tank. They called theirselves the BBQs, which stood for the Badass Bohicas prison frat and…No one had been able to come up with a good Q-word to fill-out the Greek name.

"Well, I guess this is down-the-hatch time," said Gary, holding out a grease-caked hand to shake, along with a half-full quart-size can of warm *Hairy Dog Home Brew* in the other. Leon took a big gulp and handed back the rest. "Tastes like horse piss," he said, grinning. "It damn sure ought to," said Gary, buttoning the fly of his jeans, "I had an extra-big bowl of *Stud* pills for breakfast." Everybody laughed; everybody except Sherry, who kept her head down, huffing gasoline fumes.

"Hell, it's almost time for recess," said one of Leon's closest friends, Joe Earl Somebody. "Let's go over to the junior high school and beat the shit out of some kids."

"Yeah," said another of the BBQs. "You can take on that little one again, Leon. We'll back you up this time."

Sherry's head popped up. She looked around, dazed-like. "If you do that for me, Leon, I'll let you give me a hickey anywhere you want."

"Nah," said Gary, "Leon's turned boy scout on us, aint ya, Leon. He's too pussy-whipped by that scrawny little newspaper bitch to take a chance of showing up later with a bloody nose dripping onto his Sunday-best bib-and-tucker." And that was true. Gary knew it and Leon too, even if the others were too ignorant to understand: He was gonna turn his back on the BBQs, put his hell-raisin' days and nights behind him, and join the ranks of the club's hated enemies: the goody-goody boys. Gary gave him a hard push to help him out the window and send him on his way to a brighter future.

About three hours later, Leon sat at a shiny-topped courtroom table, with his mother fidgeting in a chair beside him. A high front to the judge's bench blocked his view of His Honor who would decide his fate, and with the knees of Professor Stern pressed tight together in the witness box, he couldn't see up her skirt neither. He had told his mama about the psycho professor who had testified at Gaylord Goodhart's sentencing down in Texas, which had resulted in his high school classmate and co-hero on the football team getting the death penalty for killing his daddy, Coach Goodhart. Mama, who had always doted on him, started working a third job, sold all her furniture, even the TV, washing machine and laundry dryer, to pay for the professor to be an expert for him too.

"Mr. Corn is not a young man of bad character," the professor now said. "Indeed, never in my twenty-odd years of examining male oddballs, have I ever encountered one more lacking in any character whatsoever."

Leon's shoulders sagged. His mama stood up, no doubt to give the judge a stank-eye. "That's what I've always said," she said. "Leon is just easy for others to lead along like a mule, always into a patch of trouble." Leon hung his shaved head, as his mother started telling about his life of crime:

"Little Leon was only four or five years of age when we moved into town," she said. "A nerdy kid down the block, Jimmy-What's-His-Name, invited him to be his friend. But Little Leon, quick as a weasel, soon caught on that the Durland brat next door was king roach of the neighborhood in-crowd. He got hisself in with them by throwin' a rock at Jimmy; hit him in the head. Afterward, he was never quite right; same for Leon too.

"A few years later, that Gary sumbitch got all the juvenile delinquents into a gang, and of course Middle-Size Leon got all the way into harness. There was a rumble with another badass bunch. Leon got beer pressured to pick a fight with one of the Campfire Girls. He got his nose bloodied, and didn't even learn a lesson to always hit the other fella, or gal, first. With his no-account daddy still run-off and me workin' nights at the bowling alley, there was no one to keep Middle-Size Leon from following in the ways of bad company.

"Big-Size in high school, Leon got onto the football team," his mother continued, "but when he tried to git one of the gals—that runt of the litter with strawberry-blonde hair—she kicked him in his privates; then took up with that half-breed who moved into town, the coach's boy, Gaylord Goodhart. Oh yeah, Gaylord 'Goody-Goody' was star of the team, everybody's hero, and when he went rotten, so did Leon, even rottener."

All true, Leon had to admit. After Henryetta had played hard to get with him, he had tried to win her back by being just like her "hero." Not being half-Indian like Gaylord, he couldn't run fast; couldn't throw, catch or kick a football; but he could drink beer, smoke pot, and pick fights on and off the field for Gaylord to finish. The two of them—the "Lone Ranger and Tonto"—got permanently expelled from high school on the same day. Gaylord left town, and a year or two later got sent to prison down in Texas, but..."Big-Size Leon stayed inside the immobile house for a whole year, nursing his broke heart," said his mother from beside him. "Then Barney and me set up housekeeping, and at about that same time Gary Durland got out of prison. So Extra-Big-Size Leon..."

"Thank you, Mrs. Corn," said a deep voice from above, which must have been the judge's. "Do you have more to say in this matter, Professor Stern?"

"The mother is quite right," said the skinny, dark-haired college teacher. "Her pathetic male offspring, though surprisingly intelligent in an animal sort of way, has no moral foundation under him; he will go in the direction of the strongest gust of wind. For instance, though his disgusting heterosexuality is tightly bound, and made rabid by long-term ingestion of testosterone supplements, such is his penis envy for this Gaylord Goodhart—whom I happen to know a great deal about—I have no doubt Mr. Corn would readily enter into a flaming homosexual relationship with his hero if so blown. Goodhart and this Henryetta person are virtual doppelgangers in his severely roided-up mind."

"Doppelgangers? Surely you don't mean those German dogs."

"Not necessarily, your Honor. I mean only that Mr. Corn sub-consciously perceives the 'hero' and the 'girlfriend' as virtual doubles."

The judge's voice made a hmmm sound. Leon began to

worry. "Sounds to me like Mr. Corn belongs in a loony bin 'stead of prison. And after all, as to the charges against him, there was no penetration of the victim, only dry humping. So…"

"Ordinarily, I would agree," said the professor, "but as you may not be fully aware, the Oklahoma state prison is in the process of becoming an enlightened institute of correctology, under the auspices of a noted colleague of mine, Doctor Frigg. True, though highly regrettable, OIC will continue to field a so-called bigtime football team for the smalltime being, but If anyone can squeeze the testosterone out of young male brutes such as Mr. Corn…"

"But I understand there are to be women admitted to the new OIC," Leon heard the judge say, which was news to him. "I worry that they may be in danger from…"

"As you said, your Honor, Mr. Corn has been charged only with humping," Professor Stern pointed out, "and I doubt there will be livestock inside the walls. Women are most in danger of sexual assault in their own homes by legal hetero spouses, unless sensibly single and well armed."

"Good point, Professor Stern," said the judge's voice. "As a matter of fact, I have here a letter from this same Miss Henryetta he's so stuck on. It's a character reference submitted to the Department of Corrections at the defendant's request, but…let's see: In answer to being asked to evaluate his character, she put a big 'X' in the box marked 'Bad', and added the word 'VERY' next to it."

Leon's heart skipped a beat. Henryetta still cared enough to write a letter about him.

"And as to whether he should be given another chance to do right, she checked the 'No' box and put down an exclamation mark so hard it poked a hole in the paper."

Leon almost swooned.

"Miss Henryetta then goes on and on, using both sides of the page, with reasons the defendant is more than deserving to be sent to…That settles it, Mr. Corn. I hereby sentence you to three years of correction on the rock pile down there at the Oklahoma Institute of Correctology! Court adjourned!"

Both Leon and his mama stood up. Both speechless, they hugged for the first time since he'd gone off to kindergarten. Hot damn! He wasn't dumb like a fox; he was smart as that other b'rer in the book he'd read in high school; the one who threw the pesky rabbit into a briar patch. The very thing Leon had most wanted was to get into OIC, where he would be a football hero; graduate; and come back home to put a hickey on Henryetta's neck.

FIVE

Having semi-lied to her mother, Wynona Sue, that she was working on a "Lifestyle" piece for *Femichismo!* about hot new hairdo trends of importance to women, Henryetta semi-slunk through the back door of the Best Little Hair House, with pad and pencil in hand. Though she had practically grown up inside the beauty parlor, watching her mother cut, curl and dye ladies' hair, in a hallway leading from the back door, she right away noticed a "roach" she had previously overlooked: From back in the 1950's when the parlor was a plain ol' barber shop for men, an old cartoon—enlarged and still plastered to a wall by coats of clear varnish—showed a man's head sticking through a doorway to what must have been a similar hair-cut shop, asking: "Bob Peters here?" A figure of a barber, at work on a customer setting in a chair, answered: "Nope, just shaves and haircuts." And though the picture didn't clearly show any skin color of a smaller figure kneeling to shine the customer's shoes, from the back of his head it looked to Henryetta like his hair was at least semi-nappy.

Fired up to stomp a foot, Henryetta went on into the main

parlor room. In answer to her asking her mother what she had to say in defense of the oldtime picture in the hall, in particular its offensive display of one of those down-putting racial stereotypes…"Wynona Sue woulda yanked that man inside <u>by</u> his 'Petie'," said one of her co-workers, Ms. Pearl, with a laugh. "She would have 'bobbed' <u>for</u> it, alright." *Ha, ha, ha.*

"And then Wynona Sue woulda 'bobbed' <u>on</u> it," said Crystal, another co-stylist, also laughing. "She woulda threw that man on the floor and bobbed up and down 'til he cried 'Uncle.'" *Ha, ha, ha.*

Henryetta's mother, Wynona Sue, and three middle-aged gals in chairs getting hairdos, laughed along with Ms. Pearl and Crystal. "Write down 'The Bob' for your article, Henryetta," said her mother. "That's the only 'lifestyle' trend that'll always be hot in these parts." *Ha, ha, ha.*

As she jotted notes, Henryetta realized that gals had always jabbered like that in the beauty parlor; about how to get a man and what to do with him. Yep, right on cue: "I told her," said Ms. Pearl, "'Honey,' I said, 'if you wanna git Floyd Davis to notice you at that dance club up in Tulsa, just let me put a little pink in your hair, maybe some neon purple to perk up the pistachio. You don't have to put an ink tattoo right there between your ta-tas. After you git 'im, you can go back to dishwater blonde'."

"Aint that the truth," said Crystal. "No right-in-the-head woman would put a particular color to her hair if she knew she was never gonna get to change it."

"Just what I always told Henryetta, didnt I, Honey," said her mother, Wynona Sue. "A cute blouse with leprechauns on it might be your favorite, but you wouldn't wanna have to wear it everyday for the rest of your life. Men don't marry and stay married to gals with tattoos all over 'em."

"Especially if the 'leprechaun' was tattooed next to her 'pot o' gold' by name, say, 'Patrick', and now she's got a Charlie searchin' for that 'end of the rainbow'." *Ha ha, ha.*

"Men notice women's hair, Henryetta, not color on their skin, 'cept a little above the eyes, cheeks, lips," said Crystal. "That's why I always advise against shaving and waxing, you know, down there in the crotch." *Ha, ha, ha.*

"It's true as a trivet," said Ms. Pearl, a gal semi-older than the others. "My ex, Joe Bob, told me that back in the day, when he used to take his sack lunches to strip clubs to get out of the sun, the thing that would get a gal yanked off the dancin' pole quicker than green grass through a goose was if she flashed any of that unpublic hair outside her g-string. The very sight of it is what gets a he-mouse up on its hind legs, roarin' like a lion." *Ha, ha, Ha.* "Joe Bob used to say that if not for that patch of fur down below, there would be a bounty on women." *Ha, ha, ha.*

"Well, I won't color a bush, not even my own," said Crystal, a dishwater blonde, "unless a fella wanted me to do it for Cinco de Mayo or somethin." *Ha, ha, ha.*

Ignoring the ongoing ladies lip music, Henryetta took stock of the beauty products lined up on glass shelves below the long mirror they were all lookin' at theirselves in. Sure enough... "How come you don't have no *Bronzer*, no *Midnight Magic*, no liquid *Colortration*?" she asked her mother.

"We don't have much call for those here at the Hair House," Wynona Sue answered, without a speck of shame on her colored-up face. "Why are you askin' about 'em, Honey?"

Henryetta stomped a foot, and shouted: "'Cause a black gal, who didn't see the 'sign' that might as well be stuck on the front door, could come in here wantin' a beauty treatment, that's why!"

"An albino black man was here just yesterday, askin' for those very products," said Ms. Pearl. "I steered him to Beulah's over in Okmulgee."

"Henryetta, you know very well all the black gals go to Beulah's Beauticious Bootyque," said her mother. "I go to Beulah my own self when I want sparkle on my nails and eyelids."

"Which is when Wynona Sue's on the prowl up that way," said Crystal. "It's dark inside Roxy's Clam & Salad Bar on 'All The... Free Ladies... You Can Eat... Nights'." *Ha, ha, ha.*

"You'da thunk Rocky woulda got around to straightening out that sign by now." *Ha, ha, ha.*

Henryetta was in no mood for funnin'. "Maybe African-American gals drive all the way to Beulah's 'cause that's the only place where they get treated decent," she said to Wynona Sue's face, "and don't have to hear the hurtful N-word."

"N-word?" said Wynona Sue, like she had never heard the term. "Why, I never..."

"Beulah's is where you're sure to hear that particular N-word flyin' through the air like pots 'n' pans," said Crystal, laughing. "Usually when she's bitchin' about the no-account men in her life, which is <u>always</u>." *Ha, ha, ha.*

"I used to use the double-N-word on Joe Bob when he went to gettin' in my hair," said Ms. Pearl. "N-N-for-numb-nuts, which is French for the D-word: dumbass." *Ha, ha, ha.*

Henryetta stormed out the back door of the Hair House. Marching at a furious pace back to the *Weekly Herald* office, she set her mind to composing piece for G.G. Carpenter at *Femichismo!* as follows: *Any woman wanting, say, a Bob job done on her, would do better to not stick her head into The Best Little Hair House of this Oklahoma town. On the other hand, anyone looking for roaches in cracks...*

At her *Weekly Herald* desk fifteen minutes later—after

processing a short morality tale on her computer and sending it to G.G. Carpenter—Henryetta began to cool down. Among all the foul things that had come out of her mother's mouth through the years, the N-word was not one of them that she could rightly recall. Wynona Sue her own self had once been engaged to marry a dark-skinned "Rajah," who she thought was from India. She got all the way to Atlantic City, New Jersey with him before finding out that his prior references to "Lahore" weren't about his mama—who she was traveling to meet—but about his hometown in Pakistan; and that his name was Punjabi instead of Rajah. Also, after Gaylord Goodhart—the love of Henryetta's life—went away, and she started going with a boy named Otis, who was African-American...Yes, it was true that Wynona Sue just about ran Otis out of town, but only by pestering him so hard to marry her daughter and set-up housekeeping locally.

And now Henryetta also recalled that Ms. Beulah her own self had a foul cartoon of sorts in the ladies room at her Beauticious Bootyque that was worse than the one in the Hair House hallway. Years ago, before she was a teenager, her mother had took her in there to "powder their noses." She'd heard Wynona Sue giggling in the stall, and then saw with her own eyes an old photo on the wall above the commode. It showed a black man—with a wicked alligator-size grin on his face and nothing on the rest of him—standing under a palm tree. Someone had wrote on the picture: *Wish you were here, and I bet you do too! Love, Sis.* At the bottom of what must have been a post card, a printed caption said: *An' there we spied...*

Only now, more than ten years later, was Henryetta shocked to have seen the N-word in writing, but there it had been, right in front of her: An *"N-word with a trigger that was bigger than an elephant's proboscis or the whanger of a whale."* A footnote identified the rhyme as from a book, *Grapes of Wrath,* by a man named John Steinbeck. She'd later heard about him, only a couple of years ago. He was the book writer who made up the term "Okies" for her own people—choked by dust storms and having no jobs—who went out to California to work stooped-over in fields, picking vegetables.

Henryetta now felt ashamed to realize that the same man who had created the complimentary word "Okie" for red-dirt folks like her—that she had been proud to carry her whole life—had also put down in writing the N-word. And she was disgusted too that women the age of both Wynona Sue and Ms. Beulah cared less about racism roaches on their own premises than about men's "whangers."

SIX

Standing in front of a full-length mirror mounted to a wall in his OIC quarters, Coach Charles "Buster" Downs — in a skimpy, skin-tight wrestler's singlet such as he almost always wore — took a deep breath; squatted; hoisted a hundred pounds of iron to his midriff; and started a repetition of curl lifts. One, two, three... The workout between morning and afternoon football practice sessions was his way of relieving stress in advance of his mother's daily phone calls. His mom and he had been especially close in his youth; staying in touch allowed her to re-live those glory days, in which she had re-lived her own prior feats in the wrestling ring. Back in the late 1960s, his mom — known as The Human Ball Buster — had dominated the unisex circuit until taking a Flying Scissorkick to the forehead from Cowboy Bill Watts that fractured her skull. Following his birth, she had devoted herself to being coach and trainer to him — Little Buster — on the junior unisex circuits. He'd known a father only by name: "Artie" for artificial insemination, but...forty-eight, forty-nine, fifty.

Coach Buster dropped the weights onto the padded rubber

wrestling mat covering the floor of the largish room that served as both his office and living quarters. As taught by his mother — "Keep 'em in the cup," she constantly lectured — he adjusted the stainless steel shield inside his jockstrap that protected what she called "the family jewels." His mom had been a real father to him as he grew in height and width — even now to barely over five feet tall by barely under five feet across — and became known, first as the The Little Dough Ball, then The Human Meatball, then The Human Bowling Ball, and later, after he turned professional, as everything from the short-fused Human Cannonball, to The Human Wrecking Ball, Gutter Ball, Oddball and so on; only to be unfamously remembered on the unisex circuits as The Human Foul Ball. His mother had taken the hardest fall for his careless mistake in the ring during a mother vs. son exhibition match at the Mom's Day *Slammeramamama* charity event in Las Vegas, where and when…

At the painful recollection of being booed off the mat for an attempted Organ Grinder move from a Hopping Bunny position that had gone terribly wrong, Coach Buster again adjusted his jockstrap containing the stainless steel cup that he absolutely always wore; then squatted and again hoisted the weights. One, two, three…

Luckily, he had been able to get a job as locker-room janitor at Murray State, only a junior college at the time, located in Tishomingo, Oklahoma. Over a period of almost twenty years, he had been promoted up the ranks of the football coaching staff, until being named head coach of the Alfalfa Bills just as Murray State achieved university status and committed itself to playing bigtime college football. Very luckily for him, a kid named Gaylord Goodhart — who turned out to be the greatest college football player in history — showed up on campus with a buddy,

Billy Ray Williams, who also made All-American as a wideout receiver. Danged if the Fighting Alfalfa Bills didn't beat the University of Texas Burger Kings for a national championship, in a match-up that turned out to be the last bigtime college football game ever played. Bigtime prison football had won the hearts and minds of kids, fans and TV marketeers by then. So he'd thought he was a third time lucky when he got hired to coach the OSP, now OIC Wild Bunch. But with his first season on the job coming up, now he wasn't so sure he hadn't crapped out. A new female Dean…

At the sound of his phone tone playing the tune of *M is for the many things she taught me* spells M-O-T-H-E-R song, Coach Buster dropped the weights to the mat and adjusted his cup. It was his mom, of course, making her daily call from the Retired Rasslers Home out in Los Angeles, California.

"Buster, you will never guess who I saw rassle at the *Great Balls of Fire* event on pay-per-view last night," she said. "Cowboy Bill Watts, who now calls himself Grandpa Bill, in a steel cage, no-holds-barred match against Babs 'The Human Bimbo' Brogan, who was never strong enough to carry my jockstrap. She got lucky and put a Reverse Bucking Cowgirl move on Grandpa Bill. They gave her a belt with diamond-studded buckle. Dang! If I could get over these headaches; if the UWF would let me out of that lifetime ban, heck, on the senior unisex circuit I could…" As his mother carried on with her regular woe-is-me, what-might-have-been tale, Coach Buster put his phone on speaker mode, laid it on his desk; adjusted his cup and went back to pumping iron.

Coach knew his mom meant no harm; in her eyes he was still her "little medicine ball of muscle" she had thrown around the ring in his toddler years. Long ago she'd forgiven and forgotten his "miscue," but still his mother seemed to always bring up something to remind him that he had disgraced both himself and her, resulting in their joint exile from the world of unisex wrestling. He had meant no offense; it was an equipment malfunction that had brought their Mom's Day match to its embarrassing termination, not to mention the end put to their good standing in the Unisex Wrestling Federation. He had simply intended to make a perfectly legal move on her, but…Dang it! His old singlet tore, his jockstrap loosened, his cup slipped out of position. The next thing he knew, his mom and him were being dragged out of the ring, pelted with boos and popcorn from the offended crowd of mostly mothers and children. As a minor, he'd been put on probation for misdemeanor "flashing," but his mother had been charged with corrupting his morals and insulting community decency standards and manners.

"Buster, you were lucky to get out of that Humping Camel Ride the prexy at Murray State had you in," she now said, changing the subject of her conversation to his narrow escape from the unwanted attentions of the female president of Murray State. "Like I always told you: Don't ever let a woman get the top position. And that is exactly what they are all doing these days on college campuses coast to coast."

With him semi-listening, his mother went on to tell news about male-and-female goings-on at an Occidental College, located near the Retired Rasslers Home. She re-reported that last year a boy-and-girl pair of students out there got drunk; did the Dirty Dance move in his dorm room; and that after leaving, she called to ask if he had a condom; then came back to do the whole Love Hug. A week later she said she didn't remember what happened, except that she got raped. So they kicked the first-year boy out of the college. And now, according to his mother, for all institutions of higher learning out there, the State of California had made up a new law that would make an illegal Man Trap move out of a pre-match handshake: "'No' means 'No'" was not the rule no more; and "Yes" didn't necessarily mean "Yes" no more either, unless an accused male could prove a gal's "affirmative consent" at every step of the match; which would be impossible to do if she claimed she was drunk at the time.

"And everywhere else the Feds have got colleges in a choke hold with the muscle of something called 'Title IX', Buster," his mom said. "To run off all the red-blooded jocks, they've set up kangaroo courts, just like the Unisex Wrestling Federation did to me. So your lucky to be off that Murray State campus, and in prison; safe from one of those dirty Fainting Fox moves aimed at drawing a foul call against you. If only I could get out from under this UWF ban and..." The phone at the old rasslers home started clicking to signal that his mother's allotted time had about run out. "But just in case, Buster: Keep 'em in the cup."

Buster dropped the weights and adjusted the stainless steel protector of the family jewels inside his jockstrap; thankful that the new female Dean of OIC—who was his boss—wouldn't be able to put one of those muscular Title IX college choke holds on him.

SEVEN

It was almost noon the next day when Henryetta got back from Okmulgee. She'd drove her Checker up there earlier to compare goings on at Beulah's Beauticious Bootyque with those the day before at the Hair House — they were exactly the same — and on account of Mr. Shat's need for a wig freshening product, she had asked what would be the best thing for jet black, frizzy hair. "I reckon the best thing would be to dye it blonde," Ms. Beulah had said. "Men don't get up on their hind legs for black-haired women." Feeling personally offended by the racist comment, Henryetta had set her own self down in a Beauticious Bootyque chair and told Ms. Beulah she would be much obliged to get one of those jet black Afro hairdos. Now, walking into the *Weekly Herald* office, from the back of his own frizzy black-haired head, Henryetta saw that the man settin' across from Mr. Harold at his desk, though dressed in an orange outfit, was Mr. Shat.

To judge from the jaw-dropped look on her boss' face, Mr. Harold only semi-recognized her in her new do. "It's me alright," she said, moving closer, "it's your protege, Henryetta." Mr. Harold stood up, like he was going to put out his hand for a semi-formal introduction or somethin'. "Well, I declare," he said, before sweeping the arm around and turning his wide-eyed gaze toward his old college friend and colleague. "Henryetta, I'd like for you to meet Mr. Jamus 'Sheep Dog' Murphy from Peterboro, New Hampshire. He's passin' through town, and dropped in to say howdy." Land sakes alive! Mr. Shat's face and ears and neck and hands had turned dark brown!

"It's Shat!" Mr. Harold blurted, as if the skin color difference would have fooled her. "Call me Sheep Dog," said the famous reporter, also standing up as if to meet her for the first time, then eyeing her up and down like he was fixin' to herd her into a sheep pen or somethin'. "Looks like my great mind, and yours too, Loretta, have been thinking alike: Both determined to walk the walk in African-American shoes," he said, settin' back down, "so we can honestly talk the talk about what it's like to be an oppressed victim?"

"Shat, I mean…" Mr. Harold lowered his voice to continue: "I mean Sheep Dog here, is going in the hole, Henryetta; he's gettin' into the cracks of a big morality tale for the *Weekly Herald*, like another fella did back in about 1960 so he could write a book he titled *Black Like Me*." She had never heard of such a book, of course. So her educated boss explained that a white journalist had dyed his skin back then in order to feel, and write about, what it was like for a black man to take a six-week bus ride through deep southern states.

"I get it," said Henryetta, turning to Mr. Shat's dark brown face. "That's why you were wantin' a jar of that *Bronzer* cream or *Colortration* at the Hair House. Where'd you find it? Even Beulah's Beauty Bootyque up in Okmulgee didn't have none."

"Had to settle for Oil of Shinola," he answered. "Scored ten gallons at that shoe repair factory down by the railroad tracks.

And by the way, Harry, I insist on picking up the tab for a new tub in your guest bathroom, unless you and the Missus think a plain white replacement would now clash with the slightly stained tile floor."

"I get it," Henryetta said again. "You're gonna walk around in a black man's shoes, and skin, to see how it feels. But why not do it in your own name, 'Shatner Lapp'? Not many folks except me and Mr. Harold have likely heard of you in these parts."

"Shat's got a new angle," said Mr. Harold, semi-whispering. "He's going to take the real Jamus Murphy's place in prison down in McAlester."

Prison?! Henryetta was struck speechless. "But...but...OIC is for youngish folks twenty-five and under," she finally said. "They've made the prison into a correctology college."

"No, I read they have a few spots for left-over inmates. And Shat got an idea for a big story on a bus bound for...You tell it, Shat, in that original way with words of yours."

"Right, Harry. And you might want to take notes, uh, uh..."

"Henryetta, spelled with a y."

"Right. Well, first let me get into the moment. Hmmm. Okay, here goes a rough draft of a preface to the series," Mr. Shat said, before leaning back in his chair and closing his eyes. "One night a couple of days ago, on a bus bound for nowhere, I met up with a stranger. We were both too tired to sleep. As we took turns passing his bottle back and forth, memories seem to overtake him. And as he stared out the window into the darkness, he began to speak..."

As Henryetta scribbled in her notebook, she began to think she must have read the book, *Black Like Me,* after all, or..."Did they ever make a country-and-western song out of that morality tale?"

The tale teller's eyes popped open. "Good idea," he said. "You're right, Harry, this girl...how did you put it? Oh yeah, she's sharp as an acre of onions.

"Now, where was I?" he said, re-closing his eyes. "Oh yeah, the stranger said his name was Jamus 'Sheep Dog' Murphy, born and raised on a farm near Peterboro, New Hampshire. At a young age, he had gone bad, and lived the next forty years of his life drinking, gambling, whoring, 'til finally, for committing petty crime after petty crime after petty crime, he ended up behind bars. After a few years in stir — that's what cons in prison call prison, 'stir' — even the screws at New Hampshire State Prison — that's what they call the guards, 'screws'----didn't want to have anything to do with him, just like his own mother. So they had shipped him out to the stricter, more brutal penal system of Oklahoma; paid thousands of dollars of taxpayer money to get him off what was left of their cold-hearted Yankee consciences. He'd begged for a last opportunity to see his dying mother on the way, and now he was on the lam, by bus, bound for nowhere.

"After I drank down the last swallow from his bottle, the night got deathly quiet. My fellow traveler's face lost all expression. He crushed out his cigarette and faded off to sleep. He'd said the best a man could hope for was to die in his sleep; so, searching his jacket pockets for the name of a next-of-kin to call, just in case, I confirmed that Jamus 'Sheep Dog' Murphy was indeed dead. No doubt he would not have wanted his also dying mother to spend her burial savings on him, I decided; which was one of the reasons I got off the bus in Bowling Green, Kentucky, and sent his body on to nowhere. Only later, in possession of all his papers and some of his clothes, did it occur to me that I might get on another bus, to Oklahoma, and continue on in Jamus

Murphy's stead; take his place in the Oklahoma State Prison, pay part of his debt to society and redeem his soul by telling a powerful morality tale from the perspective of an oppressed black man <u>inside</u> the walls."

Henryetta started not to get it. "Why re-write the book, *Black Like Me?* from inside prison walls?"

"The Old Black Joe story needs a fresh shine put to it," Mr. Shat a/k/a Sheep Dog said. "'Martin Luther King, Junior has faded to gray in the public's mind." According to Mr. Shat, newspaper editors had found it harder to make readers feel sympathetic to African-American men. The market had become saturated with competition from other unworthy minorities; the civil rights narrative had got muddled, he said. For an African-American President and First lady to say they had been insulted in their younger years to be mistook for employees at a Hilton Hotel and Target store, in jobs that men and women from Mexico, not to mention single white mothers and teenagers, would have been proud to have, made black unemployment seem somehow less tragic.

"And now it's the damned feministas who have taken over the never-ending story," he said, with sparks of fire in his blue eyes. "Those bitches—that's what they call themselves, they admit what they are—have stolen the African-American birthright to victimhood with hysterical cries of 'Rape! Rape! Rape!' on college campuses across the land. At Duke, the University of Virginia, and everywhere else, white male jocks and frat boys have replaced long dead slave owners—George Washington, Thomas Jefferson and Massa Robert—as model villains. The news media are buying it like free pussy!"

"Shat's angle, the title of his series is...You tell her, Shat."

"*Raped Like Me* is my title for the series, and book; somewhat in the vein of the best seller I wrote about a certain little trip I took from Selma to Montgomery, Alabama. I'm going to take back the forgotten narrative, tell the tale of an African-American man..."

"You're gonna go in the prison and get yourself raped in the hole?"

"Well, I am going to <u>report</u> rape in narrative journalistic style. Starting tomorrow, I will experience firsthand the context and psychological trauma of that odious crime against humanity by empathizing with its victims; putting myself in their doggy-style position and the reader 'there', in the 'moment', by writing the classic narrative on scraps of toilet paper. It will take stones alright, but you gotta have a pair to practice the art of narrative journalism, and I've got 'em; avocado-size. Right, Harry?"

"That's where you come in, Henryetta," said Mr. Harold, looking eager as a cocker spaniel dog to please his hero. "Shat needs for you to be his 'ho', right, Shat?"

"Right, Harry, to get the written tale past the screws and into publication while it's fresh, I need to have a regular visitor come see me in the privacy of the room for conjugal visits. And you would have to do some, uh, editing, Henryetta. You could be a footnote to the glory of a Pulitzer Prize."

That did it. "I'm your ho for the job," Henryetta said, feeling that she was finally on her way to understanding what it took to be a famous journalist.

EIGHT

As dear old Harry Mixon and that feisty girl at the wheel of a Yellow cab continued to nervously jabber, Shat felt uncomfortable; not *per se* about his mission to check-in at the Oklahoma state prison, called OIC. *Au contraire*, he was keistered to the hilt with mini-bar bottles of hooch; eager to get inside the walls for a massive dump of *Wild Turkey* bourbon. But he'd never been one to complain. Having to smuggle essential supplies past prison guards in a body cavity, as well as ride in the back seat of the bus on a bumpy road, were only preludes to the many hardships he would endure for the next two or three weeks in the shoes of an oppressed African-American male. Exposing roaches of racism in grimy cracks was the job of an investigative journalist, a calling for only the few and the brave to be all that they could be. As one of the unfortunate downtrodden himself, he had voluntarily enlisted long ago in the cause of championing underdogs. Born…"Arghhh!"

"Are you okay back there, Mr. Shat? That was an old tire I ran over."

Born Shatner Lapp Jr. to parents of Dutch descent—in

Pennsylvania's Amish Lancaster County, not on Philadelphia's upscale Main Line—he had been underprivileged. Even as a baldfaced white boy he'd experienced the humiliation of seeing his mother publicly listed by name on the third and last rung of the country club's curling team. His father, a socially and no doubt professionally clumsy proctologist, had sent him—oh no, not up to Groton, then on to Harvard—to the lowly Lawrenceville School in New Jersey, then to nearby Princeton; both all-male enclaves at the time. He'd not measured up to membership standards of the elite Princeton eating clubs—no Ivy Club bid for the Dutch kid from Amish Country—so had been reduced to sharing meals with other bottom rung SMOCs—small men on campus—once known as the "Sour Balls" of Tiger Inn.

"Arghhh! "

But the upper-class WASP power structure had not been able to keep him out of the prestigious University Press Club. By God-given merit alone, an original way with words, he had overcome the many blackballs dropped on his application, and begun his climb out of the trash heap of history. His regular columns about various aspects of campus life for *The Daily Princetonian*—**Shat on Sports**, **Shat on Clubs** and the like—had been popular and influential. His piece, **Shat on Women**, was instrumental to forestalling their admission to Princeton until after his departure, and to their exclusion from Tiger Inn for more than two decades thereafter. Not that he personally bore any ill will toward split-tails back then. *Au contraire* again, hobble-de-gee with members of the fairer sex was his college major. His senior paper, **Shat on Ali McGraw: Wailing at the Picture Show,** won the coveted Tiger Inn Barf Cup that year. No, it was not until marriage to a woman reared its ugly…"

"Arghhh!"

"Sorry again, Mr. Shat. But this is the only road from the turnpike to OIC, and we're almost there."

His first wife, that bitch, Brenda…No, that witch, Wanda, was the mother of his now oldest mistakes. And he'd not learned from experience; that was the worst part of his memoir-in-progress, **Shat on Himself.** If only he had heeded his barber's words of wisdom when he was single again and working for the *Washington Post.* "Marriage is like a bath," Shat now recalled Nino "Grease" Manelli saying, "after awhile, it aint so hot." So what did he do? Feeling frisky one weekend after consuming a boatload of oysters on the Maryland Eastern Shore, he eloped with Grease's ex-wife, that pig, Estelle. And later, after years of working his way through a veritable all-you-can-eat buffet of bearded clams, he had fallen for that slut, Gigi, his protege at the time. Since Gigi, there had been not much passionate hobblin', gobblin', snarlin' under the covers; only the occasional bumpin' big uglies with females whose names he couldn't recall. So, if anyone were to accuse him, Shatner Lapp, of being a hater of women, he would readily admit…"Arghhh!"

"We're here, Mr. Shat, at the Oklahoma Institute of Correctology. Welcome to your new home!"

"Shhh! Henryetta," dear old Harry commanded. "It's 'Sheep Dog Murphy' we've hauled here, and only for a short stay; right, Shat?"

With the girl—Etta Somebody—holding one of his elbows and dear old Harry Mixon the other, Shat duck-walked toward the high whitewashed walls of Oklahoma's "Graybar Hotel," a prisoner's term for his temporary accommodations. Inside an entrance to the "con college"—another convict term he'd looked up for narrative color—Etta chatted up a chubby young African-American woman, "Demoana," whom she seemed to know from a past encounter. At a check-in counter, a clerk with uncoordinated eyes—who should have been named "Igor"—looked both down to Jamus Murphy's transfer papers and at the same time up to him. "Well, well, well, the famous Sheep Dog Murphy from New Hampshire," he said. "Never thought a butcher like you would have the cojones, and lack of brains, to show up for your third degree punishment after graduating prison back east. How they hangin', Sheep Dog?"

"Butcher?" said Etta, now standing beside him. "Oh yeah," said the clerk, "the State of Oklahoma is gonna make a tidy sum for puttin' Sheep Dog Murphy's sweetbreads on the Death Row barbecue grille."

"But...but...but..." the girl stammered.

"This here is not Sheep Dog Murphy!" dear old Harry blurted.

"Says right here he is," said the clerk, pointing at the papers on the check-in desk and looking sideways at the same time: "'Jamus Murphy is hereby assigned to Death Row at the Oklahoma Institute of...'" Shat, with his one-of-a-kind nose for news of human interest smelling a bigtime roach within reach, shushed both dear old Harry and the girl before either could scare it back into the cracks of OIC's Death Row, no doubt a dank dungeon teeming with specimens of racial bigotry; and relatively safe from actual sexual assault. With his wits sharpened for the hunt, "May I introduce my spouse, uh, Henryetta, spelled with a y instead of an i," he said to the clerk. "During my no doubt extended stay on Death Row, awaiting the dreaded executioner's song, she will be making regular conjugal visits to keep my spirits..."

"Nope," said the clerk. "No conjugatin' visits for you, Sheep Dog, not 'til your day of reckoning."

"But I'll be old and ugly by then," said the "wife," that zesty little minx, Henryetta, who unlike dear old Harry was indeed sharp as an acre of garlic; and more like himself, with her own pair of avocado-size doodads, figuratively speaking. "Can't you make an exception since Sheep Dog hasn't officially checked-in yet," she cooed. The chubby African-American girl, Romona, came to Henryetta's side. "Let 'em have a little tickle, Eddie Ray," she said, "which will apt to be their last, since no one never gets executed no more 'til thirty years of appeals run out of juice."

"Well, I dunno," said the inn keeper, with a zesty leer in at least one eye toward the spicy little black-haired, blue-eyed slice of snapper, Henryetta. "Aw, c'mon, Eddie Ray," said the helpful young black woman, with a giggle. "Take 'em on over to the conjugatin' room and stand guard at the door. I'll do business for you here 'til you get back."

Down a corridor, at a pink door signed *Conjugal Visits/ Couples Only,* dear old Harry grabbed the knob, but…"Why don't you go on into town and chat with that local newspaper friend of yours," said Henryetta, handing over a set of car keys to her boss. "This might take, oh, maybe an hour or so." Eddie Ray a/k/a "Igor" licked his lips. A hairy ear twitched.

Hot damn, whatta Tiger Inn guy she would have made! The last ballsy young person he could recall having any contact with was an undergraduate president of the old college club, who he'd bumped into back in the day at Grease Manelli's barber shop in Washington. The baldfaced lad had been charged with the duty of leading dear old Tiger Inn's last ditch stand against a feminista's legal challenge to its right to remain studly stag. A different undergraduate of female persuasion had been quoted in the *Post* to the effect that she didn't think women would want to join Tiger Inn even if allowed, since "all they do at parties is get naked, get drunk, and barf on the floor." But the young Tiger sitting in the barber shop chair for a Grease job had told *The New*

York Times: "If the court lets them in, we plan to treat women the same as the guys." Ah, you could tell the young stud had been bred with a healthy pair of groin organs. Yeah, the feminista won the court battle, but as for the war: According to what Shat had heard about the current campus scene in general, split-tail members of dear old Tiger Inn must have embraced the club's manly tradition of dancing naked, getting drunk and barfing on the floor. Schweet!

Inside the dingy room for couples-only coochie-coo… "What in tarnation!" said Henryetta, stomping a foot on the grimy linoleum floor. "You never said Sheep Dog Murphy was a butcher, sent down here to Death Row for a third degree!"

Shat suggested she turn around and close her eyes; dropped trow and squatted his big be-hind over a wastebasket. Ridded of his supply of *Wild Turkey* bourbon by massive dump of contraband mini-bottles that inevitably would have been discovered prior to his admission to the no doubt exclusive Death Row Club, he pulled up his orange pants and washed his hands at a free-standing lavatory. "I didn't know Sheep Dog was an oppressed and <u>condemned</u> black man," he then explained. "Schweet! "

"<u>Was</u> Jamus Murphy African-American?"

"Who's to say he wasn't. The important point is that my **Raped Like Me** morality tale now has a dramatic life-and-death backdrop," Shat explained to the young small town reporter, "making it much more yeasty."

"But how are you gonna get the story out of Death Row on toilet paper?" she asked.

Hmmm, and how to get mini-bottles of booze in? Shat had to think about that for a second. "Piece of cake," he then said, reaching into a pocket for the quarters he'd intended to use for bribing prison guards. "Come back down here tomorrow, or later today to meet another con in this little love nest," he said, while pouring the quarters into a wall-mounted vending machine. "Give him a glimpse of your ta-tas, ride a leg—that's a prison term for non-sexual sucking up—maybe put an innocent lip lock on him and make him our mule."

"Mule?"

"Put the whip to Old Dobber's tokhis," he said to his ho, handing over the packets of condoms he had bought with his bribe money. "Give these love sheaths to the mule. Have him get them to me on Death Row. I'll pack 'em with installments of my morality tale and he'll keister 'em out to you here, in the private couples-only room."

A ceiling light began to blink off-and-on, indicating their allotted time for zesty ingus was up, Shat thought. An aroma of fried bacon wafted into the room through its AC ducts. "Schweet!" he said. "Smells like I'm just in time for brunch at The Graybar."

NINE

After giving "Sheep Dog Murphy" a peck on his brown cheek and taking her leave of him, Henryetta found her way to the old football field inside the walls, where Demoana said the OIC Wild Bunch team was practicing for the upcoming season. She had been there before, back when prison football was about to put bigtime college football out of business. The *Weekly Herald*, being a newspaper from a small town not far from the state penitentiary, had been asked by *The New York Times* to send in five hundred words about the Wild Bunch, and she, the *Herald's* so-called sports editor at the time, had drove down there to interview the head coach, D.C. Cantwell, who…Dang it! As it later turned out, he was the no-account sumbitch who tried to "recruit" Gaylord Goodhart—still the love of her life—by framing him for second degree penal penetration of a barroom floozy down in Tishomingo, where he was set to play ball for the Alfalfa Bills of Murray State University.

By coincidence, the current OIC head coach was the one who Gaylord finally played for at Murray State. Semi-exaggerating that she was a *Times* reporter, she had interviewed him too, along with a tall and lanky ol' gal who was a kind of "sexy prexy" of the university. And now... Henryetta found Coach Charles "Buster" Downs standing under goal posts at an end of the field next to an upright blackboard; wearing a skin-tight rassler's outfit; still a block of muscle, squared off at the top by short sandy hair standing straight and lined up even as the mowed lawn of a country club.

"Oh yeah, I remember you," he said, after she'd stuck out a hand and re-introduced herself. "You're that newspaper gal who used to have different colored hair, and got Gaylord Goodhart out of that fix down in Texas. Has that New York City paper sent you down here to do a story about this year's Wild Bunch?"

"Not exactly," she said. "I got a note about a player from a little ol' town up the road, name of Leon Corn, and just came by to see how he's doin'." And that was semi-true. The card she'd got from Leon just three days before, thanking her for her "Letter of Recommendation," had printed on it a *Hallmark* sentiment—*I Know You're Not Right for Me, But I Can Change*—and Leon had wrote by hand that he was gonna make her proud by being a football hero at OIC. So to the coach, she said: "Leon Corn is what you might call a local hero that everyone's bound to be real proud of when he becomes a star player for OIC."

"Corn, you say?" he replied, looking down at a sheet of paper on a clipboard. He turned the page with one of his stubbed-off fingers. "Nope, no Corn on scholarship as of now."

"He just got here and might have walked on without a pre-set scholarship."

"Hmm," hmmed Coach Downs, turning more pages and looking up and down at the names on them. "Nope, no Corn listed," he then said again. "What position did you say he plays?"

"Oh, he's a... a Studback, like Gaylord Goodhart, but better,"

Henryetta answered, looking down the field toward a bunch of players, all of them black as far as she could tell. "Leon is white, very white, with red hair."

"A Studback better than Goodhart?!" Coach put a set of binoculars up to his eyes. "Only white boy out there is that big'un we've got playin' the blockin' dummy position."

He handed the spyglasses to Henryetta, who put them up to her own eyes. A "blocking dummy" in a white numberless uniform got up from bein' knocked down, rassled the helmet off a smaller black player, threw him to the ground, and commenced to stomp on his head. "Yeah, that's Leon alright," she said, "and yeah, all the oldtimers up there in Hotagg…"

"Hotagg? I don't recall ever hearin' of…"

"H-o-t-a-g-g: That's what they call the little ol' map dot of a town at Exit 237 on the Interstate—for 'Hometown of Troy Aikman and Gaylord Goodhart'—and the oldtimers up there say Leon Corn is a better Studback on two legs than the two of them together on four."

"Well, I declare," said the coach, running a hand across his flattop, "I'm in sore need of a Studback, that's for certain. I'll put Corn on scholarship soon as I…"

"You may have to sweeten the pot to keep him," said Henryetta, who had learned a thing or two about the ins and outs of bigtime prison football recruiting in the past. "'Cause I hear the Texas State Penitentiary is tryin' to get him for their Chain Gang team, just like they stole away Gaylord from the Oklahoma Wild Bunch before he ended up at Murray State."

Coach Downs' ears turned from resembling raw cauliflowers to looking like boiled red beets. "Sweeten the pot? I can't pay out cash money, the NCII has got strict rules about that kind of thing now," he said, referring to the National Conference of

Inmate Institutions that governed bigtime prison football. "But dang it, I sure could use a blue-chip Studback of Corn's caliber."

Henryetta opined that Leon was a true red-dirt Okie at heart, who would no doubt druther be a star Studback for the Wild Bunch, if only…"Only what?" said the coach, looking like a bigmouth bass ready to jump into her boat. "If only he could get a cushy job of some kind," she continued. "Maybe one that wouldn't require him to study too hard on his rehabilitation, and not tire him out too much to practice football every morning and afternoon. Maybe Leon would be satisfied if all he had to do between practicin' touchdowns was, oh, I don't rightly know, maybe push a meal cart up and down the corridor of Death Row, where it's likely to be quiet and restful," she said, just as a plump, middle-aged gal in a pinstriped jumpsuit—sorta of a younger Hillary Clinton in big-bottomed shape—walked up next to Coach Downs. She introduced herself to the football coach as a Dean Frigg.

"*New York Times*!" she said, after Coach Downs had semi-misintroduced her to the Dean as a special correspondent. "You shouldn't be talking to <u>him</u>," she said, without even a nod at the football coach. "<u>I</u> am in total control here at the Institute of Correctology."

Henryetta got a pad out of her jeans pocket and a pencil from the one on her shirt. "How many condemned men have you got on Death Row, and how long do you reckon it will take to get to the last one in line?"

"Death Row?" Dean Frigg covered her mouth and turned to Coach Downs. "About fifty," he said, "all past age of eligibility to play. Most have got old waitin' in line for the needle, and now the engineers are havin' trouble gettin' the new electric chair powered up to snuff."

"Electric chair?!" said the Dean, obviously surprised to learn she was in control of such an apparatus. "Over my dead body!" she then said to Henryetta's face. "Any such dunce's stool in detention hall is simply too cruel and unusual for me to contemplate, or to have to watch, much less pull the lever of an electric chair. I don't think I could ever recover from such cruel and unusual trauma. Better that a thousand butchers go free than to chance taking the life of an innocent killer."

Glad to hear that Mr. Shat was safe in that regard, Henryetta went to her next question: "What are you doin' to protect the inmates from rape?"

"Inmates? Rape? Oh, you mean homosexual sex," said the Dean. "Well, I'm afraid there's nothing I can do about that. Some boys <u>will</u> be boys, and some girls will be girls; they are born that way. I myself am pro-choice. However, editors at *The New York Times* can rest assured that once the young women arrive to make this a co-educational institution, I will put forth and strictly enforce rules and procedures for their protection from unwanted heterosexual sex! And you may quote me on that."

To clarify what she reckoned Dean Frigg must have meant to say, Henryetta omitted the word "unwanted" from the quote she jotted, and took her leave of Dean Frigg and Coach Downs.

TEN

Upon her realization that OIC was a penal rather than academic institute of correctology—some two hours after her arrival onsite—Ester had taken herself and Martha Washington to her "Dean's" bed. For two miserable days and nights, they had wept and cuddled between intermittent fainting spells. Only this morning, awakened by the sickening smell of fried bacon, had a more profound realization come to her: By declaring the prison to be an institute of correctology and accepting federal funds for this-and-that program deemable as educational in nature, the feminist Lieutenant Governor of the State of Oklahoma had effectively handed the Governor's swollen male head to the U.S. Department of Education on a platter. By phone, a nameless bureaucrat in Washington had confirmed her finding, had administered an oath of office; had directed her to set up an internal judicial system for resolving sex assault charges; and had effectively put her in absolute command of OIC by authority of Title IX. Thus empowered, she would be able to make her mark in the field of Correctology by putting the "pseudo-prison" on a sound and gender-just co-ed footing. While other Deans elsewhere wrestled futilely with unruly male correctees, she had hers already in chains—by the testicles, as it were—with unfettered disciplinary authority to break their individual and collective will.

And of course one of the first reservoirs of testosterone to be squeezed out of the system puddled in the jockstraps of male athletes. Already, a *New York Times* correspondent had taken notice of the so-called "Wild Bunch" football team and its coach, Mr. Downs. Soon the little black-haired *Times* reporter would have real news fit to print. Having marched to the football practice field—now standing beside the coach at a blackboard marked-up with diagrams—Ester moved in for the first squeeze: "Hmmm, 'Q-Back'," she said, referring to a notation on the blackboard. "Very good, Coach Downs, though of course we will have to verify this designated participant's sexual orientation to determine eligibility. And here," she said pointing, "I trust your 'H-Back' is also Homo, not Hetero."

Coach "Buster," no doubt already feeling her subtly applied pressure, nervously adjusted the codpiece of his ridiculous skin-tight bathing suit dating back in style to the nineteenth century. "You see, Coach, federal guidelines and my own preferences require equal opportunity and diversity of participants," she continued, while looking out to a squad of brutish, armor-clad football players comprised almost entirely of young African-American males.

"You mean I gotta play... please, not women. Dang! Ms. Frigg."

"I'll get to women later," she answered. "But do my eyes deceive me or is that a white person out there on the field, bullying that underprivileged black one?"

"Oh yeah, that's Leon Corn; he's reputed to be diverse as a

one-man band. You know, like you see on street corners: Foot workin' a drum; knees bangin' cymbals together; arm slidin' a trombone. Corn's our new runnin' and passin' and kickin' Studback, though so far he hasn't shown much…"

"Exactly; he is a pathetic example of 'not much' diversity. I want to see yellow 'Studbacks' on the field or…Is Mr. Corn a Muslim, by any chance?"

"I couldn't rightly say, but he comes from a little ol' town north of here, so he's more likely Baptist."

"<u>Christian</u> Southern Baptist?" Ester was aghast. "My Goddess, I hereby declare Mr. Corn to be on probation, ineligible to participate in extracurricular activities until he has satisfactorily completed my correctology class on Sensitivity Training." Her subordinate again adjusted the bulging codpiece and looked up to her, his mouth agape. "Surely you know what I'm talking about," she said to the seemingly confused coach. "Even that testosterone factory called Notre Dame requires its football players—the white ones, at least—to attend such classes in order for them to understand and feel ashamed of the positions of privilege they occupy by sheer accident of birth."

"Thing is, Dean Frigg: Corn's the only blue-chip Studback I've got on roster," the physically and mentally dense ball of muscle whined. "And with our opening game against the Colorado Cutthroats comin' up…"

"You may have to cancel," said Ester, "which could be a fortuitous lightening of your workload, Coach Downs. Women will soon arrive on campus, and Title IX requires you, OIC's Director of Athletics, to organize opportunities for their participation in healthy physical activities equal to what is afforded to male correctees."

"Women? A Wild Bunch of women wouldn't have a fart's

chance in a windstorm on a football field against the Cuttthroats!"

"Forget football. You must offer our women opportunities to recreate as members of, oh say, dodgeball, ping-pong, darts teams."

"I wouldn't recommend darts, Dean Frigg," he said, literally squirming to protect his testicles. "And I don't rightly know how to coach ping-pong or...or nothin' else that don't take muscles!"

With Coach Downs reduced to clutching his crotch with both hands, Ester marched back to her residential office in the Dean's *nee* "Warden's" House. There she found Demoana Somebody—a young, overweight African-American woman whom she had promoted to Assistant Dean—still pecking at a keyboard. "The sexual conduct rules can wait," said Ester. "Get one of the small blackboards I provided and take down more dictation. The time has come, as the Walrus said, to talk of many things," she added aimlessly, before clearing her throat to begin dictating orders.

"Walrus? Is that wth a capital W, Dean?"

"No, my dear; that was just a line from a silly poem that came to mind," Ester explained. "Take down this: Effective immediately, football practices shall be limited to thirty minutes a day in order to allow sufficient classroom time for correctology instruction on the subject of..."

"Uh oh. Better not do that, Dean," her assistant presumptuously advised. "Peoples all over the state take their Wild Bunch football serious as measles, especially the Governor, who..."

"Nonsense. People used to take football seriously at Harvard too, and unlike the Ivy League colleges, I doubt OIC has many rich and powerful alums to grumble about football's de-emphasis in favor of academics."

"Like I says, the Governor…"

Ester ignored her assistant, finished dictating her football order, then shifted her weight in The Big Dean's Chair to the other cheek. "Now, for the next batch of gonads, those dangling between frat boys' legs."

"Frat boys?" said Demoana. "You mean the Crips, the Bloods, the Aryan Brotherhood and those other gangs?"

"Yes, yes, all the 'I Felta Thighs' of whatever stupid name," said Ester. Though Harvard's all-male so-called "final clubs" represented a small fraction of its student body, their continued existence as private organizations was an insult to women on campus. But Yale had managed to rein in one or two of its most misogynistic men's fraternities, and Princeton had long ago fully integrated gender membership of its old boys so-called "eating clubs" by getting a judge to declare them "public" components of its private co-ed campus life. Ignoring Demoana's counsel, Ester shifted her seat weight again and fully vented her feminist loathing of frat boys.

"You want me to type up these right now, or finish the new sexual conduction rules? They're already up to past twenty pages and…If you don't mind me sayin' so, Dean Frigg, my mama taught me there's only one rule that works against men, and that's for gals to keep their skirts down, their panties up, and their knees together."

"Nonsense," Ester answered. "As a rule of sexual conduct, abstinence has never worked. My objective is to feminize human nature here at OIC, not criminalize it."

As a final item on her morning agenda, Ester, a devout vegan, ordered a stop to OIC serving bacon or any other products cruelly rendered from humanity's animal companions. Yet again, poor, uneducated Demoana, as if to presumptuously doubt her superior's qualifications to fill The Big Chair, rolled her eyes. On a window sill, even Martha Washington nervously fidgeted, no doubt wary—so unnecessarily, thanks to Title IX—of continued presence of menacing dogs and unwelcome tomcats on campus.

ELEVEN

At her *Weekly Herald* desk, Henryetta fired up her computer to do some research for possible sidebars to Mr. Shat's upcoming **Raped Like Me** series. Right away she found a racial angle: According to an article in *The Atlantic* by a writer named John Ford, a botched lethal injection at OIC back in 2014—when the "Institute" was called the plain ol' Oklahoma State Prison—had sparked a flare up of argument about whether a death penalty was too cruel and unusual to be allowed by the United States Constitution. Apparently the Supreme Court once must have thought death was at least too cruel if not unusual, but changed its mind in 1976. Now a new argument being made was that putting someone to death for committing a crime was unconstitutional because the condemned man—Death Row had always been a sorta old boys club—was statistically likely to be black. For Oklahoma, a chart showed that less than ten percent of the state population was African-American, but that almost forty percent of the Death Row population was, in fact, black skinned.

And those percentages were about what the national average

amounted to, though in some states the statistics painted an even darker picture of racial injustice in cases where an African-American was charged with murdering a white person. In Georgia, he would have been about 4.3 times more likely to get the death penalty than if he had killed another black person, according to a famous study. Six of every eleven defendants convicted of killing a white person back in the 1970's and 80's would not have got the death penalty if their victims had been black, the article said. Henryetta scrolled down and read that between 1980 and 2008 about half of all homicide victims were black, but more than three out of four victims of executed Death Row defendants were white. Henryetta reckoned that to even out that injustice on the victim side would require putting more black men to death for murdering their bros.

So she began to feel unmoderated by Dean Frigg's claim of having total control of OIC, and about Mr. Shat's well being on Death Row. By dying his skin with Oil of Shinola, he might have cut in line and got ahead of white men who were more deserving, which even she knew was not the kind of affirmative action the Reverend Sharpster was always yellin' about on TV. And to make the death penalty even crueler and more unusual… Henryetta set to researching use of the electric chair to kill oppressed African-American men.

She found out that Thomas Edison, the founding father of electricity, was hisself against the death penalty that was carried out back in the early 1900's by hanging or firing squads. But in greedy competition about whether his DC power ideas were better than a Mr. Westinghouse's preference for AC power for general use—called the "War of Currents"—to illustrate how dangerous the AC type could be, some of Edison's assistants made a movie, titled "Topsy," that showed a Coney Island circus elephant get killed by a bolt of AC. The DC PR backfired on Edison. People got to thinking that Westinghouse's AC power could be applied to lots of useful things, including chairs wired to electrocute criminals, mainly murderers. Pretty soon lots of states installed "Old Sparkys" in their prisons. Alabama called its chair "Yellow Mama," 'cause it was decorated with a cheerful color of paint they had on hand for striping roads.

Just as Dean Frigg had done when describing the cruel and unusual trauma she her own self would experience pulling the power lever of an electric chair, Henryetta shivered as she read about the ghastly procedure of death by electrocution: Condemned men had their heads shaved…They were put in diapers before settin' down in the chairs…By all accounts their jerking when they got the shock of lifetime was a dreadful sight to see…In at least one case of electrocution, down in Florida, flames shot out of a condemned man's head. Thankfully, most states later went to more humane, less unsightly use of lethal injections, though some still allowed for electrocution as an alternative in certain situations. A lot of other states did away with the death penalty by any means, and in others that still had it on the books, such as California, no one had been officially killed by a prison warden, or "Dean," for years. Nebraska was the last state to use the chair exclusively, up to 2008, when its own Supreme Court declared it to be unconstitutional.

Henryetta specifically Googled *death penalty in Oklahoma*. She read that since 1907 her home state had put almost two-hundred criminals to death, about half mostly by electric chair and the rest by lethal injection. She went to another news page and…Uh oh.

In a tizzy after reading a recent newspaper article from the *Tulsa World*, headlined **MAMA MEGAWATT TESTS**

AT OIC HAILED AS PROMISING, Henryetta started frantically typing what she prayed would not turn out to be a sidebar to Mr. Shat's obituary:

Local folks who don't read Tulsa and Oklahoma City newspapers may not be aware that a new high-powered electric chair called "Mama Megawatt" has been installed at the state prison in McAlester, newly named the Oklahoma Institute of Correctology. This action follows a recent unanimous decision by the United States Supreme Court declaring that a death penalty by electrocution is not necessarily cruel and definitely not unnaturally unusual if carried out in comfortable upholstered recliner chairs sufficiently powered by environmentally friendly windmills. So far, volts and amps generated by wind have failed to reach a humane level in tests on pigs. However, Lieutenant Governor, Priscilla "Prissy" O'Fallon hailed ongoing progress and ordered that the engineering and testing process be expedited to ensure "our state's continuing economic development through interstate commerce."

Under a new federally funded program called No Inmate Left Over ("NILO"), Oklahoma has taken the lead in promoting interstate...

By the time Mr. Harold got back from his weekly Odd Fellows lunch meeting in Okmulgee, Henryetta was worried sick that Mr. Shat had got hisself into trouble deep as a grave. "We've gotta hurry down to McAlester and get Mr. Shat off that Death Row," she yelled at her boss, waving a print-out of the sidebar she'd wrote. "The State of Oklahoma has gone into the electrocution business down at the correctology institute. They're fixin' to fire up an electric chair and kill oppressed black men for profit."

"What in tarnation!" said Mr. Harold, setting down at his desk and taking off his Odd Fellows aviation cap and hoodwinks. "We started using uncruel lethal injections years ago, Henryetta, even though the dang lawyers make a death penalty so expensive. There's no profit to be made in it, and Shat is not really…"

Henryetta took a deep breath, tried to moderate herself, and explained that under a federal NILO program, states such as New Hampshire — that wanted to get rid of hardened criminals but didn't have the stomach for carrying out death penalties their own selves — were allowed to transfer prison inmates to other states such as Oklahoma, that got thousands of dollars in federal money for doing the ghastly deed to inmates of all ages. That explained why the otherwise youthful OIC had admitted Mr. Shat. "It's one of Al Gore's ideas for showing how booming a green economy can be," she reported. "More federal money is being sent down here for windmills to generate electricity for a new chair and…"

"Well, there you have it," said Mr. Harold, waving her out of his face. "These alternative energy experiments never pan out. Experts say that if all the cockamamy notions did work, perfectly, they wouldn't replace as much as one percent of fossil fuel use. And besides, Shat's not…"

"One percent would likely be enough to do the job on poor old Mr. Shat," Henryetta argued. "They're roastin' pigs down there right now to test Mama Megawatt, and our Lieutenant Governor says…"

"Prissy O'Fallon, 'Mama Megawatt'?"

"No, that's what they're callin' the new high-powered electric chair, named after an old cartoon character named 'Reddy Kilowatt', and…"

"Oh yeah, I remember that little rascal. His face was a socket and his arms and legs were bolts of electricity. He was an advertising logo for…"

"Well, Mr. Shat is in danger of having electric bolts shoot up his own legs, and set his head on fire if we don't hurry on down there. Oppressed black men like 'Sheep Dog Murphy' don't stand a chance against the likes of a Mama Megawatt."

"Murphy wasn't African-American, and neither is..."

"Who's to say he wasn't? Mr. Shat's goose could get cooked, God forbid, if Sheep Dog Murphy's victim was white."

"Well, some of them likely were..."

"Some of them! Oh no..."

"...most sheep are, though of course..."

"Sheep?!"

"That's what Sheep Dog was sent to prison for in New Hampshire: Rustling sheep and butchering a few of them. I reckon Oklahoma wouldn't execute a man for such a crime, even if Al Gore favored it. Cattle rustlers maybe, but sheep...? And anyway, Shat may be black-skinned now, but actually he's Pennsylvania Dutch; and I've got his get-out-of-jail identification cards right here in my desk drawer for whenever he wants 'em."

Henryetta's worry statistically moderated some. On top of Sheep Dog Murphy's victims not being white-skinned people, like Mr. Harold said: Mr. Shat wasn't really African-American. On the other hand, according to a "Murphy's Law" she'd heard about, if things could go wrong, they likely would go wrong.

TWELVE

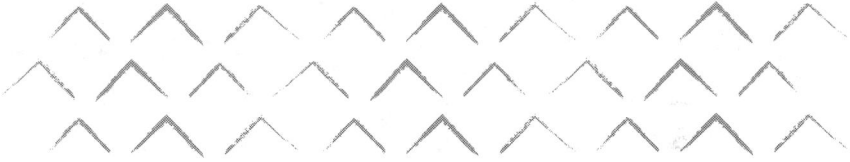

As had become his habit in grade school, Leon Corn went to a back-row desk in an OIC classroom, and slouched into a chair. All the other guys in there were also football players and... Reminded that his eligibility to become a football hero depended on getting a passing grade in "Sensitivity Training," Leon straightened himself. At the front of the room a woman with a hair ball on her head was writing with chalk on a blackboard: D E A N F R... A light-skinned black guy came in and tapped her on a shoulder. "Sorry, Dean Frigg, I chopped down a tree to get this one for you," he said, handing her a polished apple, "and I cannot tell a lie." She told him to set down, and he came to the only desk still not took, on the back row next to Leon. "Hey, you're the white blocking dummy, right?" he said, putting out a hand to shake. "I'm Buddy Brown, wideout, honorary OIC trusty, president of the bird watchers club and..."

"Quiet!" Miz Frigg shouted. "Sensitivity Training shall now begin!" Leon got a pencil and a wadded sheet of paper out of a pants pocket, as the teacher started to teach: "In this class, during the coming days, weeks and possibly months, you males shall be disabused of the misinformation, misconception and misogyny upon which your self esteem is misplaced. Today, I shall begin to pry open your minds, not to mention your testicles, with an introduction to what we shall be discussing as I drain the swamp. I refer of course to injustice to women routinely inflicted upon us by men in this patriarchal system you have wrought."

"Pssst," hissed the brownish guy, Buddy. "'Misogyny' means you hate women." He was so smart, he wasn't even writing down notes of what the teacher was saying: "To get the balls 'roiling', so to speak, consider this: Without clearly distinguishing unempowered women—whom I shall hereafter refer to as 'mice'—from empowered women—whom I shall refer to as 'cats'—studies show that women are moodier, more inclined to depression, and generally less happy than men—whom I shall hereafter refer to as 'dogs'. This grave injustice cannot be justified, of course, but what could possibly explain it?"

"Men need only one pair of shoes and one wallet," said Buddy Brown, without even bothering to raise up his hand first. "Women, like my mom, and my aunt have bunches of…"

"They would be mice," Miz Frigg replied. "Good point, Mr. Brown."

"And men only have one hairstyle for a lifetime, not like women who…"

"Unempowered mice again; yes, they change hair color and cut to attract and please the tastes of dogs. On the other hand, cats…"

Sick and tired of his classmate getting all the brownie points, Leon vocally volunteered that women had it worse than men because they had to wear shirts, and not just to family funerals. She ignored him, and kept on going back and forth with the bird-watching club president about the unfairness of men's underwear at six bucks per three-pack, about women getting lied to by auto mechanics, about men with gray hair and wrinkles bein' considered good looking, about mice giving up their names in marriage and having to be pregnant, etcetera and so on.

"And men don't have to shave their legs and armpits," said Buddy Brown Noser.

"Another good point about mice, Mr. Brown," said Miz Frigg. "The 'need' of such practice is an artificial construct of the patriarchal society in which women suffer; however, I assure you that but for the constraints of my pantsuit I would show all of you dogs fulsome sprouts of female hair, thick and lustrous as that of Martha Washington."

Leon rose out of his chair. Hot damn! Miz Frigg was hot! "Pssst!" said the class brainiac, reaching across to restrain him. "She's the wife of George Washington. Make a note."

Dang it! Leon got back on his feet to make a point: "Dogs relieve theirselves anywhere they want to, but women have to get in line to the ladies room and wait their turn to set down on the toilet."

The teacher gave him a funny, narrow-eyed look. "Quite right, Mr. uh, Corn. In fact your observation is pithy with good points." Leon set and stared down 'Mr. Brown', as Miz Frigg went into a long lecture about a classic example of injustice to all women, both mice and cats: Long lines to female "necessary rooms" at intermissions of symphony concerts. With lots of mentions of a feministical writer named Ms. Chemaly, she said that women needed to use bathrooms more often and for longer periods of time—in and out of more cumbersome clothes than men wore—to do things like change tampons, take care of children, even breast feed little ones, and…"Primp in front of big mirrors," said Buddy Brown. "My mom goes in there to put powder on her nose, and doesn't come out for hours."

"Shut up, you little twit!" the teacher shouted at him, before going on to say that more and bigger public rest rooms for women were not an efficient and politically practical way to wipe out toilet injustice. Unisex rest rooms worked better, she said, and would soon be put into operation at OIC. Women would have a Title IX right to cut in front of men in shared waiting lines. "But that alone will not be enough to solve the problem," said the Dean, "which brings me to what Sensitivity Training is all about: Correction of insensitive male behavior! Now, there once was a time when well behaved males stood when a lady entered a room. Why would that almost certainly not be the case if, for instance, I walked into a unisex necessary room today?"

Before Buddy could beat him to the draw, Leon shouted, "Because then I would likely turn around with my fun gun aimed at you, and would fire a barrage of used *Hairy Dog Home Brew* out of my bladder onto your shoes."

"And that would not be polite behavior," said guess who?"

"Wrong, both of you. Except for Mr. Brown perhaps, most males would not politely "stand" because <u>they</u> <u>would</u> <u>very</u> <u>likely</u> <u>not</u> <u>be</u> <u>sitting</u> <u>in</u> <u>the</u> <u>first</u> <u>place</u>! The patriarchal construct of males standing to urinate must and shall be eradicated. As has already been adopted into law in some European communities, henceforth at OIC any male found guilty of such behavior shall be severely shunned. All of you shall be trained to become what in Germany are called *sitzpinklers*. Given that women—those usually burdened with the chore of cleaning up bathroom drippings—were as one in demanding such legislation, some hard core masculists, who refuse to sit, derisively use the term *sitzplinkler* to describe such male kind as "hen pecked." I say, so be it! Indeed, I can think of no greater example of injustice to women than…"

As the teacher continued teaching, Leon, eager to become her pet, blurted: "And split-tails gettin' humped from on top is another good thing for dogs that cats and mice on the bottom probably don't like."

Miz Frigg gave him another one of those squinty-eyed looks. "Another good point, Mr. Corn," she said. "You refer, of course, to the so-called 'missionary position' for conduct of sexual intercourse, doubtlessly so named as metaphor for the subjection of female natives of other countries by patriarchal Christian missionaries. We shall discuss such matters in future classes. For now, suffice it to say that when I am finished with you, none of you dogs shall ever again 'hump' any kind of female from on top! Class dismissed."

As Leon and the other football players headed for the door… "Mr. Corn, I must have another word, in fact several more words with you," said Miz Frigg. He went up to her, expecting to get a gold star. "By letter from a dear colleague, Professor Stern, I am informed that in addition to being white you are particularly over-supplied with testosterone, and thus are a danger to the female co-eds who will soon arrive on campus. Extra Sensitivity Training is clearly called for in your unfortunate case."

She then picked up a stick of chalk, went to the big blackboard and began to write on it: *This is my penis, it's not a gun. It's only for peeing, not for fun.* Then the teacher turned, handed the pink chalk to him, and gave instructions: "While repeatedly reciting this simple lesson, you are to write it on the blackboard as many times as possible; erase the board and repeat the process until you have etched the rule onto the board and into your psyche by a thousand repetitions. This shall be your thrice-daily exercise until further notice. Understood?"

Leon took the pink stick and began to chalk and chant: "This is my penis, it's not a gun. It's only for peeing, not for fun. This is my penis, it's not a gun. It's only for peeing, not for fun. This is my penis…"

"Good, very good, Mr. Corn," said his teacher from behind him. "In time, I shall squeeze every ounce of testosterone out of you. You shall be the goody-goody poster boy for the benefits to be achieved through properly applied feminist correctology."

"…not for fun. This is my penis…"

THIRTEEN

Henryetta checked in at the OIC conjugating room admissions desk. The same clerk who had ushered her and Mr. Shat into the quickie love nest—"Eddie Ray," according to his nameplate—ogled at her with what seemed to be one good eye. "Like I told you and your condemned black fella before," he said, "no more conjugatin' privileges 'til his judgement day." She told the sumbitch she had come to visit a different inmate, name of Leon Corn. "Oh, you're a hot one, aint you?" he said, with a slyer look in his other wandering eye. "Have an itch for bad boys, do ya?" She shook a fist at the no-account clerk, which set him to thumbing through a list. "Oh yeah, Corn," he said, before looking back up at her. "He just got put on the blue-chip list. Temporarily on probation from football, but lucky for you, he's still eligible for poontang privileges. Go on in there and get yourself lathered up," he said, with a nod of his bald head to steer her. "I'll have the Studback fetched by the time you're good and ready."

The wretched "hook-up" room for inmates and their wives or girlfriends—that she'd took no notice of during her prior visit—was furnished with a single wood chair and a sagging bed covered by a ratty spread. On a wall for decoration, inside a pink outline of interlocked hearts, someone had wrote by hand a verse of poetry that was semi-sweet:

THE BED MATTRESS IS FILTHY WITH MOLD
BUT JUDY JUST HAD TO GET POLED.
AND WAS NOT SO VERY PARTICULAR.
SO I STOOD HER UP
AGAINST THIS WALL
AND DID IT TO HER PERPENDICULAR.

Dreading her duty to see Leon for Mr. Shat, Henryetta paced the gray linoleum floor. Back in tenth grade she had fought off Leon's advances at her by grabbing the crotch of his jeans and squeezing hard as she could 'til he cried "Uncle." Years later, she had let him know that "no means no" by givin' him a cheerleader kick to his gonads that had set him to yelping like a freshly "fixed" tomcat. That was when the sumbitch came back from Gaylord's trial down in Texas to gloat that Gaylie, the love of her life, had been found guilty of killing and dismembering his own daddy, Coach Goodhart, which turned out to be an untrue hoax for gettin' Gaylord into the Texas State Prison to play football. And since then Leon had semi-stalked her off and on.

She wasn't scared to meet up with him, not exactly, but he had always been inclined to act specially crazy when roided-up on body building pills, and even from a distance on the football practice field the other day, he looked like he'd got big as a house. Leon's recent greeting card said he could change, and that he was gonna make her proud by becoming a football hero, but Henryetta was inclined to doubt OIC was likely to achieve such a miracle of rehabilitation. Jealousy of Gaylord was at the bottom of his crush on her, she reckoned, which itself was crazy as a Betsy bug in a way. 'Cause as it turned out, the love of her life was gay as a flower garden. Now Gaylie and a Murray State team mate, Billy Ray Williams, were a same-sex couple; both playing ball for the Dallas Cowboys. As for her own unlove life…

Leon stormed into the conjugatin' room, wild eyed and drooling. Henryetta took hold of the wood chair to fend him off. "Down! Down, Leon!" she barked. He lunged at her. In self defense, she kicked him in his personal dish of prairie oysters. Just like years before, he went to mewing like a pussy cat. "You had no call to do that, Henryetta. You, your own self invited me to conjugate with you, and I've already started to change into a football hero like Gaylord, but not the homosex kind. Dean Frigg has started my rehabilitation, teaching me all about words, American herstory, and… Dean Frigg says I can fit in on campus and get eligible again if I mind my manners not to sex assault no one and become a minority member. All the coolest frats are rushing me to join 'em, not the black-balled white Aryan Brotherhood, but the Phi Lamda stamp club, A.D. Club and original Badass Bohicas."

Henryetta put down the chair. Leon seemed sincere. She had half a mind to believe he might be able to change into someone other than his own self. "Okay, Leon, here's your chance to prove your good intentions," she said, taking Mr. Shat's packet of condoms and two mini-bar bottles of Who-Struck-John out of her jeans pockets and tossing them onto the bed. "All you have to do is take these here rubbers and…" Instantly wild eyed and beginning to drool again, Leon unzipped his fly. Henryetta grabbed back the chair. "No, Leon! No!" she demanded. "Put it back where it belongs!"

The would-be raper looked down at his pecker, already

beginning to wilt. Like a Catholic schoolboy, made to recite Hail Marys for misbehavin', he began to chant: "This is my penis, it's not a gun. It's only for peeing, not for fun. This is my penis, it's not a gun. It's only for peeing, not for fun. This is my penis…"

Henryetta reckoned there was no tellin' how long he might've gone on like that if she hadn't made him stop. "Good boy," she said, after he had zipped up his pants. "Now, see here, Leon," she then whispered, "if you haven't already got assigned to a cushy job on Death Row, Coach Downs promised me that you are gonna get put there. All you have to do…"

"I know," he whispered back, grinning: "Just put food trays through the bean holes to cells, then come by later with the cart and take 'em back through the bean holes. I did it this morning and almost everything came out okay."

"Good, very good. Now, the only other thing you need to do for me is sneak these little bottles into Sheep Dog Murphy's bean hole, then pick-up fresh-filled rubbers one by one when he shoves them back out at you in installments."

"That's so gay."

At the sound of the check-in clerk's heavy breathing at the door, Henryetta looked at her watch and hurried on: "The condoms will have secret messages in 'em, wrote on toilet paper. They're chapters of an important story Mr. Murphy and me are writing together. After you've, you know, smuggled them out of Death Row in…a body cavity, and took 'em out of the condoms, you can bring the toilet paper messages to me in your pocket when I come visit you again."

"You're comin' back to visit me again? Gosh, Henryetta, are we goin' steady like you and Gaylord used to do? Can I make a hickey on your neck too? Please."

Henryetta began to actually weigh the proposition put to

her, but…Praise the Lord, the admissions clerk busted into the room. "Time's up!" he said, looking as disappointed as Henryetta was relieved that no sex assault was happening on Dean Frigg's "campus."

FOURTEEN

Shat a/k/a "Sheep Dog" paced back and forth in his Death Row cell, a half roll of toilet paper trailing behind. While waiting for a mule to show up to take delivery of the first installment of his morality tale—and bestow a much needed mini-bottle or two—he proof-read yet again what he had already written and edited by hand on the thin tissue:

RAPED LIKE ME
by
A Blackfaced Man

I am a poor black sheep who has gone astray. Baaa, Baaa, Baaa. I am a sacrificial lamb facing judgement day. Baaa, Baaa, Baaa. An oppressed black soul in Cell Block D, doomed from here to eternity; Lord, have mercy on such as me. Baaa, Baaa, Baaa.

In other words, I am living the misery of an oppressed African-American man, condemned to die and already half buried under a mound of dirt covering the top and three sides of Death Row inside a certain institute of correctology that I dare not name. Twenty-three hours a day, seven days a week, I am confined to this dank concrete cave measuring 8' X 12' X 8'; furnished with a built-in concrete cot, lidless crapper for a bedside table of sorts; a single lightbulb mounted to a wall. I occasionally glimpse natural light, but only through a slit in the steel door of my cell across a corridor from a dirty window. Unfresh air is pumped in by an antiquated AC system. Prison guards, called "screws" for good reason, regularly piss in the ducts, filling my cave with their stench. But that's not the worst of my degradation at the hands of the Mighty Whitey injustice system of this country; not by a long shot.

Thirty minutes ago, the hacks—that's another apt term for the guards—dragged another oppressed black man down the corridor outside my cell. He squealed like a stuck pig. Oink, Oink, Oink. Now the bare bulb in my cell blinks off-and-on as he sizzles in the high-voltage embrace of Yellow Mama, which is what condemned black men call the electric chair they recently installed down the hall. Oink, Oink, Oink.

Ah, the smell of fried bacon, you might say; and I'm told it's true that cooked pork tastes a lot like scorched human flesh. The very thought almost ruins my appetite for ham. Tomorrow or the next day or the next, the bosses—another colorful term for guards—will come, hopefully first for my bro, Rabbit, then perhaps for my bro, Greasy from two doors down, then for my bro, Big Tuna, and finally…They say, ask not for whom the oven timers in our cells next blink to announce that another of us will soon be medium-to-well done. Most of my nightmares are about Big Dick Bob—that's what we cons call the unpatriotic bastards who move in on our hos outside the walls—but sometimes in my tormented dreams comes the bitter-schweet smell of lamb fries roasting on a campfire. Baaa, Baaa, Baaa.

In the distance, I hear the lonely wail of a passing train's whistle as another Old Smokey comes 'round the bend. No doubt rich white folks are sitting in the bar car, drinking whiskey and smoking big cigars.

But not yours truly, not this oppressed black man. I'm headed nowhere except down to Fire Lake. They say I have it coming, and maybe that's true. I shot a ewe in Reno just to watch her die. But as the Hallmark greeting card company says: "Each man kills the thing he loves." Baaa. Baaa. Baaa. Sure, when I hear that train whistle blowin', I hang my head and cry. But don't feel sorry for me. I begged to be sent to Death Row to escape the constant sexual harassment I suffered in the general prison population. When I got to my new cell in this rancid place called The Hole, I shouted: "Free at last! Free at last! Thank God almighty, I'm free at last!"

Why? Why would I want to be dealt those eights and aces? Why would I yearn to walk that Green Mile down the corridor to Yellow Mama's hot lap? Why…?

At the sound of footsteps in the corridor outside his cell, Shat froze, half in terror that one of the screws was coming for a "visit," half in hope that a mule bearing desperately needed supplies approached. Warily, he got down on his knees and crawled toward the steel door of his cell. More warily, he peeked through the slit in the door intended for delivery of food trays, called a "bean hole." Mercifully, the screw with dangling nightstick passed by without incident. Half relieved, half disappointed, Shat returned to pacing and proof-reading:

Why would I volunteer for what cons call a "backdoor parole"? Because my life inside the walls was a living hell. Sure, they gave me three hots-and-a cot, which was better than I ever had on the outside as an oppressed African-American man, but at what cost? Daily degradation was the price I paid through the wazoo, by which I delicately refer to my being subjected to unrelenting sexual harassment and assault. More than <u>two</u> out of five oppressed black men on prison campuses are victimized by such brutish means in the course of chowing down half a hamburger, which is prison terminology for serving a five-year sentence. No one cares. News media don't scream hysterically about the ongoing racially biased rape epidemic in stir. The Feds have not forced prison authorities to set up internal justice systems for dealing with the perpetrators of sexual crimes against us. "Frat boys" are the worst offenders; members of the Aryan Brotherhood, of course; also the Hispanic Netas; even the Crips, the Bloods; and especially the swaggering mixed-race Badass Bohicas strut their stuff at will. Guards shamelessly enable their use and abuse of we black sheep. Baaa, Baaa, Baaa.

So yes, I sought the short-term refuge of Death Row, I asked to be dealt the dead man's hand, only to discover to my horror that for an oppressed African-American inmate there is no escape from the prison campus rape epidemic! My doodads fell from frying pan onto a red-hot grille. At this very moment, I hear the dreaded sound of a screw's nightstick raking the wall of the Death Row corridor as he stalks me in my cell. He peers through the bean hole to watch me dancing naked, which the Supreme Court has declared to be my Constitutional right. "Hubba, hubba," he says, pushing his obscene nightstick through the hole and waggling it, as though I am nothing but a sex object; as though I am responsible for his erection; as though by shaking my bare booty I have given him a Constitutional right to…I can't bear to even write the R-word, the psychological trauma is too great.

I get myself dressed, but…He's baaaack, banging on the steel door with his nightstick. I shrink into a corner of my cell. Two screws barge in, the ones with the preppy names, "Crotch" and "Quilty." Without so much as a tender word, their touching begins; up my spread legs, all over my trembling body. "You know the drill, Cupcake," one of the gangbang enablers hisses in my ear. "Strip!" The other moves behind me, nightstick at the ready. "C'mon, Big Bottom, time for your weekly *shower," he says. "Let's see what you're hiding between those bodacious buns of yours." Desperately, I hope it's all just a harmless prank, but alas, no. And so it goes, week after week. Baaa, Baaa, Baaa.*

In Death Row's communal shower room, I innocently offer to lather up the lily-white back of another inmate named Cracker. A look of depraved lust flashes in his baby-blue eyes. I turn away, but "Oops," I drop the soap. Though feeling used and dirty after another week in The Hole, I do not dare bend over to pick up the bar of Ivory. Fool me one or two or three or four times, shame on you, I always say. Fool me ten or fifteen or twenty times afterward, shame on Cracker, Rabbit, Raw Dawg, Greasy, Roach, Wolf and all the other condemned men on Death Row, more than half of whom are African-Americans, though we make up only an unfairly small percent of the national population. Baaa, Baaa, Baaa.

Back in my cell, I lie down on my concrete Cadillac ----a colorful prison term for bed—and try to blot from my memory...No, I cannot bear to even think the R...

At the sound of footsteps in the corridor outside his cell, Shat again froze, not the slightest bit in terror of a guard approaching, but with desperate hope that a mule brought hooch. Again he got down on the floor, crawled toward the steel door of his cell, and... schweet Jesus, a mini-bottle in pristine condition came through the bean hole, then another. "Mr. Sheep Dog," said a voice, "it's me, Leon Corn. Henryetta said you might have something for me to take back to her." A fresh condom appeared.

Shat put an eye to the bean hole..."Arghh!"

He rolled backward onto the hard concrete floor, traumatized by what he had seen. "For cryin' out loud, you idiot!" he yelled. "I'm not going to install my installment. That's your job! Stay where you are and wait for me to stuff it into this rubber."

Shat retrieved the toilet paper manuscript. Before rolling it up for delivery through the bean hole, he picked up his ballpoint pen and made a final editorial change, to the title:

R***d Like Me

FIFTEEN

At her *Weekly Herald* computer, daydreaming, Henryetta was eager as a new bride to get her hands on Mr. Shat's first installment of **Raped Like Me**. As she scrolled through internet stories with a "Shatner Lapp" byline on them—from *Newsweek*, the *Washington Post*, *New York Times*, *Boston Globe*, and later in his career from lots of smaller city newspapers and other mostly for-men-only publications—she could see for her own self that Mr. Shat had an original way with words and a one-of-kind nose for human interest news angles, just like Mr. Harold had bragged:

WHY DID SHE HAVE TO DIE?
By Shatner Lapp

Kids ask the darnedest questions. But the little girl kneeling beside me, still holding the barely warm hand of her mama and weeping, deserved an honest answer. Maudie Mae Crocker had to die because four score and forty years ago she had the misfortune to be born in the Deep South as an African-American slave. "Yes, Virginia," said I, "there is a Santa Claus, but he is an old white man more likely to take your toys than...

SHARING A BLACK MAN'S MEAGER MEAL
By Shatner Lapp

With a gap-toothed grin, Big Mike looked at me and said he eats roaches off the grimy prison floor for the same reason he once bit off a man's ear: "I do it for the protein," he said. But behind those gapped teeth lies a bitter truth. Mike Tyson had the misfortune to be born an African-American. He doesn't complain about his meager prison diet or harsh treatment by the guards, but if the roaches ever run out…

HE LIED BUT PROBABLY NO ONE DIED
By Shatner Lapp

Okay, maybe in his passion for racial justice, the Right Reverend James Sharpster loves personal publicity not wisely, but too well. Maybe his slightly false accusation that a white District Attorney in New York himself participated in a gang rape of an African-American virgin saint caused some damage to others. He didn't mean nothin' by spouting defamation of character so unwisely, but passionately well enough to incite widespread riots. Unlike President George W. Bush, the Right Reverend Sharpster had the misfortune to be born an impoverished rabble-rousing Little Black Jimbo with an unaffordable taste for silk suits. On MSNBC there is no shame…

COTTON PICKIN' TIME IN DIXIE
By Shatner Lapp

After totin' sixteen tons of cotton bales to the levee with my African-American brothers and sisters, another day older and deeper in debt, I wiped sweat from my sunburned brow and sliced open a watermelon. Later, I would get a little drunk and land in jail. But in the moment, looking out at Big Muddy, a new way of expressing the injustice of it all suddenly came to me: That old man river, he don't plant taters, he don't plant cotton, he just keeps rolling along...

And Mr. Shat's interview of an African-American-Russian cosmonaut was datelined MOON.

Now he'd come up with a whole new angle to the ongoing African-American civil rights story. And because Mr. Shat was limited to putting it down on wads of toilet paper smuggled out in condoms, there was bound to be a lot of editing and writing for her to do. Visions of a Pulitzer Prize footnote danced in Henryetta's head, 'til interrupted by the buzz of her eye-phone.

"G.G. here," said G.G. Carpenter through the phone. "About this piece you submitted on 'beauty parlor' racism and hair: It's garbage; not at all suitable for publication in *Femichismo!* My Goddess, what were you thinking, H.E.?"

Henryetta, took back by Ms. Carpenter's sharpish way of getting to her point, kept quiet as the *Femichismo!* editor kept on rejecting what she'd wrote.

"The <u>next</u> to last thing our readers care a fig about is more of the unending 'woe is me' complaints of oppression by black people. For the past sixty-five years, at least, that tired tale has sucked all the oxygen out of the larger, more important civil rights cause of oppressed women. You must have seen the drug-dealing, pseudo-patriarchal 'stepdaddy' of the 'Black Lives Matter' poster boy on TV. Given a mic in a spotlight, out came the oppressed black man's message: 'Burn this <u>bitch</u> down!' As opprobrium, the term 'bitch' outdates by centuries the now forbidden little n-word, as do the predecessors to 'ho'. No one in the so-called mainstream media tsked tsked at the laughably archetypal MF'er's hate speech as the 'Black Lives Matter' battle cry—'He didn't mean nothin', they said—but that's okay. We embrace our bitch identity. It's that MF'ing stepdaddy's balls that are going to be held to the fire next time. Along with those of thuggish black football players who complain about racist frat boys, while they themselves…"

As the "feminist" editor went on ranting about 1 out of 5 African-American football "thugs" brutally assaulting women, Henryetta reckoned "opprobrium" must mean hateful words, but made a mental note to look it up. And the word "archetypal" too.

"And the <u>very</u> last item on our news agenda is portrayal of our kind as air-headed ninnies, concerned with nothing but which hairdo and other 'beauty treatment' will get a man to take them out to dinner and into a bedroom. One might think 'Henryetta P. Hebert' was a <u>man</u>. You're not are you? We don't allow misogynists to vent their bile on *Femichismo!* pages."

Henryetta made another mental note: "Misogynists."

"And we abide by very strict standards of honest journalism," Ms. Carpenter continued, before Henryetta could speak up on the subject of her own gender. "For instance, you might have made the "bob peters" riff real, and of importance to women, by having one of the 'gals' actually do it, but…Surely this pathetic creature, 'Leona Lou', is entirely fictional, right? While *Femichismo!* recognizes the legitimacy of fudging facts in the right direction, this 'cartoon character' is an embarrassment to…"

"Leona Lou is real! She has feelings, and is likely someone's mother that doesn't deserve to be called a pathetic creature by anyone 'cept her own embarrassed daughter."

"Ah, I see," said Ms. Carpenter in a softer tone of voice. "Well, we all have a mother in our luggage, don't we."

Fighting off an urge to click off the phone, Henryetta continued to take instruction from the woman who was, after all, one of her bosses. The web news editor explained that *Femichismo!* only put out news stories slanted to expose something called "patriarchy" in order to inspire and empower women to fight for the feminist cause. "For instance, I myself am currently deconstructing <u>history</u> of a sexual assault in the White House by that despicable Republican President, Warren G. Harding," she said. "I intend to have him charged posthumously with rape, dug up and brought to justice!"

Henryetta had never heard of a President by that name, but recalled her mother, Wynona Sue, goin' tsk, tsk, tsk—more often outright cussing—at a Democrat sex assaulter in the White House, namely "Billy Clinton," who she had been briefly friendly with when he was running for Arkansas Governor.

"Oh yes, but Slick Willie got a pass," said Ms. Carpenter. "The National Organization of Women—I am not a member of NOW, but don't want get into a cat fight—found no fault in Hillary's running mate; in part by the irrelevant standard of no vaginal penetration in his case, except by cigar. And we do not abide the whining of bimbos either. See what I mean, H.E.? The new civil rights narrative is all about strong women such as Hillary, real bitches pushing men out of their traditional power positions and taking the big chairs at the table for ourselves."

Trying to think if she knew of any such gals, the only name that came to mind was a Mrs. Rutledge, who had recently got up in the big seat of her husband's demolition business bulldozer and knocked down the house of another gal he was shacked up with. Hmmm. Then there was that new Dean down at OIC, Ester Frigg. She seemed semi-bitchy.

"Ester Frigg! My Goddess, you've got to be kidding!" said G.G. Carpenter. "She was my roommate for awhile during our freshwoman year at Wellesley. Ha! 'Someone' got the cute idea to call us 'The <u>Walrus</u> and The Carpenter', perhaps in cruel reference to poor Ester's body size and shape. What a ninny! I heard she finally got canned by Harvard, but had no idea…Why on earth would anyone promote Ester Frigg to even a minor backwater deanship!"

Henryetta explained that the Oklahoma Institute of Correctology had always been bossed by men, and opined that Ester Frigg had pushed them out of the big chair because OIC was fixing to admit women and become a co-educational institute.

"Are you shitting me?!" was her old college roommate's reaction. "Ester Frigg in charge of a co-educational institute of correctology! That's a clusterfuck in the making if there ever was one, and sure to be an embarrassing setback for our cause. Ester is what we call, in oxymoronic terms, a 'neo-Victorian feminist'. She has no femichismo. She and her sort at Harvard for lo these many years have barely pushed the needle of women's enrollment to past fifty percent. Harvard's grudgingly established ODR—Office of Gender and Sexual Dispute Resolution—has shown no cojones whatsoever in the fight against sexual assault of women by elite campus jocks and overprivileged frat boys. My Goddess, Ester Frigg actually <u>condones</u> hetero-sex!"

G.G. Carpenter got quiet, but through the phone, Henryetta could practically hear her silently stewing.

"Holy Mama Maya," she finally said. "The Walrus is destined to become the poster beast for the campus rape epidemic happening nationwide, and Rush Limbaugh himself could not have chosen a more unattractive image of lamebrained pseudo-feminism. But we have to cover it," the *Femichismo!* boss lady added, "if only to paint a marginally thicker mustache and 'What-Me-Worry?' goofy expression on the face of her brand of feminism. I want you to imbed yourself in this 'OIC' and dig for dirt on 'Dean Frigg'."

After clicking off the phone, Henryetta realized she'd got a toe caught in a crack. Binding it on one side was her duty to Mr. Shat, who was mad at feminists for stealing the civil rights narrative. From the other side, another boss, G.G. Carpenter, was set on doing that very thing, and expected help from her: *Femichismo!'s* so-called bylined correspondent for Oklahoma.

SIXTEEN

With a weight-loaded bar bearing down across his chest, Coach Buster Downs lay pinned to the mat in his OIC quarters, breathing deeply and resting, while listening to his mother on a speaker phone. After discovering that OIC was to admit women and that he—in his mom's eyes, still her little Dough Ball—would be under and outmuscled by a female boss <u>and</u> Title IX, his mom had looked deeper into the campus rape epidemic that seemed to have started out there at that Occidental College almost next door to the Retired Rasslers Home. "Buster, don't you dare so much as look cross-wise at any of those 'co-eds' when they get to OIC, much less lay a pinky finger on one of 'em," she now said. "I can't have a second sex offense on your record, and still have a shot at gettin' back into the Unisex Wrestling Federation. I'll say it again, Buster, younger gals these days: They are badass bitches!

"These 'feminists' have about cleared the Occidental College campus of males with any feistiness to them," his mom said, "and others are kicking ass all over the country. Young studs are now protecting themselves, not only by keeping 'em in the cup, but also by strapping on mini-cameras in case of need to prove female consent to any move or hold that might leave a gal sore the next day. If you don't want to believe your own mother, Buster, just tune into the *Kangeroo Court* pay-per-view TV show and watch the videos. If nothin' else, you might learn something. Ever hear of a Sultry Saddle move out of a Kneeling Missionary position?" Coach managed to get his arms under the weight bar and his hands down to his crotch for a cup adjustment, as his mother continued their conversation.

"Badass bitches will be running the whole country before you know it," she said, "which is fine by me; 'cause their most sensible next step in that direction is to take over the Unisex Wrestling Federation. I have already sent a letter to the President, demanding that he put the UWF under that Title IX. And you can bet those feminists will get behind my reinstatement and stand up to those male sons of bitches who banned me. I'm just dyin' to get a steel plate screwed into my forehead to stop the brain drainage, so I can climb back into the ring and kick ass again. Can you imagine what a turkey shoot it'll be when all the unisex rasslin' rules get re-wrote by a UWF that is of, by and for females. I'm gonna put a re-legalized Nutcracker hold on Granpa Bill Watts, and squeeze 'til he licks my shoes and begs for mercy! I'd bring you along the comeback trail with me, Buster, except for the danger that my little 'Human Dough Boy' would be certain to get hurt.

"Wish I could chat longer," his mother then said, for the first time ever. "I've got to start getting in shape for my return to the ring. But before I go, one last word of motherly advice: Watch out for those badass feministas down there on that OIC campus, Buster. If you give 'em an opening, they will pluck the family jewels and put 'em on a spit over a hot fire. Keep 'em in the cup,

Buster."

Feeling exhausted, though he had yet to do any lifting of the weight he was under, Coach continued to lie on the mat, looking up to the ceiling and thinking about what might have been. Wrestling had always been his true love. Though his mom's comeback was probably a long shot, he had an urge to call her—for the first time ever—and beg…"Am I in the right place to sign up for football?" said a high-pitched voice from above. Coach adjusted his head alignment and…"Great balls afire!" he exclaimed, frantically reaching under the bar for his cup. "Females can't come into OIC 'til tomorrow, and are never to be allowed in here! Get off the mat!" The youngish white gal standing above him—long blonde braided pigtails made the figure look like a gal—was about his size, just as muscled, and wearing a tight black singlet same as him, but…

"They told me to check-in early," she said, holding to her position on the mat. "Based on a squeeze-the-balls strength test, they took some blood to look for testosterone; and sent be over here pending lab results. But I'm a girl alright. Wanna have a look inside my cup?"

"No!" Coach shouted. "If you're a female I don't have to let you play football under Title IX. Come to Dean Frigg's orientation assembly tomorrow in the Rotunda and sign up for ping-pong or some other all-girl team."

"Ping pong? That's for sissies. I reckon I'll just stick to wrestling."

"Wrestling?" There wouldn't be enough interest in his favorite sport for a women's team, Coach Buster thought. On the other hand, rasslin' was really more of an individual deal. Only a couple of semi-equal size participants would be needed to get a team started. In answer to Buster asking if she had any experience on the mat, the sweet-faced gal in braided pigtails said her name was Georgette; that her grandpa was Gorgeous George, and that since her toddlerhood…

"Gorgeous George! The Legend his own self was your granddaddy?"

Coach Buster was dubious. Gorgeous George was the famous founding father of professional wrestling. Back in the 1940s and '50s, he introduced the sport to TV; some said he was the reason television became popular. With his long platinum hair and glittery outfits, Gorgeous George was the semi-pretty face of the first "Golden Age of Wrestling." He was the sport's glamourous superstar even though—sorta like Mohammed Ali and other pro athletes since then—he played the braggart, the heel, the villain. His musical grand entrances in sequined capes were way before their time; along with his put-on girly ways that infuriated mostly male audiences. People came to his matches by tens of thousands, hoping to see him get beat, which was seldom. Buster had read a book about Gorgeous George: *The Outrageous Bad Boy Wrestler Who Created American Pop Culture.*

"If you are really a Georgette, I reckon you ought to know the rasslin' size and weight of your granddaddy," he said, still looking up from the mat.

"Five foot nine inches, two-hundred fifteen pounds," she answered; "three and a half inches taller and thirty pounds heavier than me. His last name was Wagner. He died in 1963 at age forty-eight: A long time before I was born; but he passed on his know-how and want-to by way of a younger mistress, my mama."

Hmmm. Wanting to believe, but unsure, Coach Buster asked: "What famous flavor of French perfume did 'your granddaddy' spray around the ring to make it nice for his matches?"

"It wasn't Chanel #5, in case you're tryin' to trick me, Coach. He called it Channel #10, and said: 'Why be half safe?'"

She went on to correctly name and describe all the famous positions, moves and holds of wrestling. She claimed she once gave Hugo 'The Human Pogo' Anderson a dose of the highly dangerous Thunder Clap, which would have been something to see, if true. In answer to him asking what she was doing time for, Georgette said she had not been in the mood to spark with a boyfriend, and that when he wouldn't take "no" for an answer she had made a Couch Bounce move followed by a Carpet Burn ride that left him impotent for life. "He called the cops and claimed I sexually assaulted him. The judge felt-up my biceps and took my boyfriend's side. We're livin' in splitsville, as far as I'm concerned."

Dang! Buster had not had a good muscular go-'round on the mat in years, but…Georgette was possibly one of those feminist badass bitches his mother had warned him to stay clear of. On the other hand, she had not yet been officially declared to be female. And anyway, did that little detail really matter? Now that he thought about it, unisex wrestling in general and his mother's career in particular had proved that in the ring, one on one, any move a man could make, a woman could usually do him one better. Heck, now that he thought about it some more, his own mom was, if anything, more of a so-called feminist than Dean Frigg bragged of being. The Dean wouldn't likely fire him; more likely she would understand and even approve if…

"Wanna mix it up, just for fun?" said Georgette, reading his mind. Coach Buster adjusted his cup and nodded yes. Georgette grabbed hold of the steel bar with a hand, and lifted two-hundred pounds of weight off his chest with a one-armed snatch. He took a standing Lollipop position. She set herself up for a Flying Frog move. "Let's rassle!" she said, before clapping her hands.

Game on!

SEVENTEEN

After re-reading the first installment of **R***d Like Me** that she had put in yesterday's edition of the *Weekly Herald*, Henryetta — stewing about how she could rightly work for both Mr. Shat and Ms. Carpenter at *Femichismo!* — found herself leaning away from Mr. Harold's old friend. His oppressed black man morality tale might be getting at least semi-long in the tooth, she reckoned. And his original way with words, not to mention the narrative journalistic style of "being there" in an oppressed black man's shoes, also now struck her as somehow off the mark. Mr. Shat writing that the Death Row guards who abused him had "preppy names" — "Crotch" and "Quilty" — and that he desperately hoped it was all "a frat boy prank," struck her as out of plumb. Plus, people said even *The New York Times* was goin' broke, and that "digital" news was the way of the future. She was still young and — though not what anyone would likely call a "feminist" — she was, after all, born a female.

And OIC's change to co-educational status might turn out to be a big story, she reckoned, especially if there really was a rape epidemic spreading nationwide on campuses of colleges that were also co-ed. Based on her own single semester over at little ol' Murray State when it was only a junior college—majoring in Remedial English to try to get a stronger grip on her grammar—sure enough, gals and guys got drunk, got frisky, and woke up the next morning with hang-overs and regrets; but no gal or guy ever got raped, far as she knew.

Having fired up her *Weekly Herald* computer and gone to the *Femichismo!* home page while she mulled, Henryetta now saw on the screen:

FRIGGED IN OKLAHOMA!
Unsafe Sex on The Plains
By G.G. Carpenter, Editor-in-Chief

Following a baby step forward by the State of Oklahoma, namely long overdue admission of women to the Oklahoma Institute of Correctology, reactionary government officials have taken a giant step backward by naming Ester Frigg to be Dean of the institute. Frigg comes to the post from Harvard, one of more than a hundred colleges currently under investigation by the Civil Rights Division of the U.S. Department of Education for failure to comply with Title IX's requirement that women be afforded equal opportunity for college education free from fear of sex. A rape culture on campus at Harvard and elsewhere is breeding a virulent STD more dangerous than any witch's brew festering in the Petri dishes of its chemistry labs. And Ester Frigg is a carrier. With her appointment, the national epidemic of this odious venereal disease (previously reported here) is bound to come sweeping down the plain in her wake to infect the so-called "high security" OIC facility located in the small town of McAlester.

Join Femichismo! in making strong protest by all available means against Ester Frigg and the neo-Victorian brand of pseudo-feminism she espouses. She and her permissive heterosexual agenda must be stopped!

Up with women! Down with penises!

Henryetta clicked <u>here</u> and found herself embedded in the *Femichismo!* archive of prior news items important to women:

DOING THE MATH by ADDITION,
not DIVISION
In High Heels and Backwards
By G.G. Carpenter, Editor-in-Chef

Larry Summers, infamous ex-President of Harvard, once publicly said that women lack aptitude for science, which is just another word for mathematical calculation. But as noted, he is an <u>ex</u>-occupant of the Harvard big chair, and an asshole. When it comes to relations with men, women know how to keep, and even the score.

Let's start with a recent White House task force study, confirming a prior online survey conclusion that one out of five college women are raped or sexually assaulted during their time on campus, and adding that only 12% of campus assaults are reported. Now let's dispense with the hate-speech math concocted by columnist, George Will, in the Washington Post: Given reported sex assaults against 96 of the 28,0000 female students at Ohio State University, Will <u>divides</u>—duh—96 by 12% to come up with total assaults numbering only 800, then <u>divides</u>—double duh—800 by 28,000 to support a fallacious conclusion that only 2.8% of women at OSU are sexual victims. Talk about war-on-women divisiveness! Both President Obama and Vice President Biden say the correct math is 20%, but they too are men who probably never had a campus jock force his tongue down their throats, so their figure is way low. Though they are politicians, probably they harbor the archaic notion that "rape" involves penetration, and assault involves absence of consent.

According to Professor Catherine MacKinnon, a woman and an expert: "Politically, I call it rape whenever a woman has sex and <u>feels</u> violated."

In <u>addition</u>, the 2007 Campus Sexual Assault Study by the Justice Department's National Institute of Justice that produced the <u>bottom</u> line — 1 out of 5 co-eds had been subjected to attempted or completed sexual assaults by force or due to their incapacitation — counted only victims, not incidences of victimhood. I myself, a single victim, was raped no fewer than two hundred times by only three of several boyfriends while I was at all-female Wellesley College. So let's do the <u>long</u> addition and set the record straight: At least <u>ten</u> out of five women on campus are assaulted, and that's an epidemic!

By the way, since the feminist faculty booted Larry Summers, the asshole's place in the big chair at Harvard is now occupied by a woman. Onward and Upward!

Wow! Henryetta her own self did some math on a calculator. After reckoning that all the gals down at little ol' Murray State — including her own self — got sexually semi-assaulted at least once during their time on campus, she went to another article in the *Femichismo!* archive:

DEJA VU ALL OVER AGAIN
The Same Old Story
By G.G. Carpenter, Editor-in-Chief

To read the actual Rolling Stone piece, **Rape on Campus: A Brutal Assault and Struggle for Justice at UVA** *— that the patriarchal mainstream media has been so picky, picky, picky about — is too traumatic for most of the millions of women who experience the same nightmare nightly. As if further validation of the feminist outcry against college jocks and frat boys were needed, the* *fabulous piece of narrative journalism by Sabrina Rubin Ederly puts the reader there, on the UVA campus, in-and-out of the tattered panties of a student named Jackie, as she experienced chapter-and-verse the all too common story. No disrespect for Ms. Ederly's reporting, but by touching all the bases of the ongoing campus rape narrative previously told by Femichismo! and others over and over and over <u>here</u> and <u>here</u> and <u>here</u>, Jackie's pitch-perfect portrayal of the classic campus rape paradigm reads almost like plagiarism.*

In unpicky summary: Jackie, a naive freshwoman among the "overwhelmingly tanned and blonde students at UVA" (read "snooty WASPS"), was lured to an upstairs bedroom of one of the upper-tier (read "wealthy and privileged") frat houses on the campus' notorious Rugby Road by an older young "Gentleman of Virginia." An in-crowd of five-to-seven males with preppy nicknames, "Armpit" and "Blanket" and the like (read lacrosse players), mercilessly raped her there for three-to-five hours on a floor covered with shards of shattered glass (read painful experience). An unbroken beer bottle came into play. Her date and another Virginia gentleman shouted cheers and instructions for doing the dirty deed to her, (mere sex object to them) referred to as "it." Jackie tells us that in the midst of her five-hour ordeal, she desperately hoped it was all just a frat boy prank (read "<u>very</u> naive"). Finally, she escaped, only to be told by three so-called friends that if she reported what happened (only 12% of campus rapes are reported) and they were brought into it, none of them would be welcome to have fun at future (exclusionary) frat house parties. She nevertheless courageously went to a UVA counselor, who offered a warm shoulder and hankie for comfort, but not a sharp knife in a clinched fist for vengeance.

Then comes the perfect moral of the to-die-for Rolling Stone story: After having no choice but to meet-and-greet her "cavalier" date on campus for two traumatic years—yes, not until she had suffered in silence through dozens of party-time weekends—could Jackie finally be persuaded to tell her story for publication. Only then was the larger point of her harrowing experience dramatized in print by Ms. Ederly. In Jackie's own words, she suffered at such length in obscurity because she "didn't know what resources" (for gender justice) were available." Why? No doubt partly because she did know that most cops are themselves armed with penises, but mainly because UVA had yet to establish a ruthless judicial system for dealing with its appalling rape culture, as glorified by it's "Virginia Gentlemen's" so-called drinking song, aptly titled "Rugby Road": **A hundred Delta Gammas, a thousand AZDs/ Ten thousand Pi Phi bitches who get down upon their knees/ But the ones we hold most true, the ones we hold most dear/ Are the ones who stay up late at night, and take it in the rear!**

With beer bottles and broomsticks in hand, Femichismo! is proud to join in the chorus of the opposing battle cry for justice in the fight against college frat boys on Rugby Road, and at other campus bastions of patriarchy:

BOHICA! Bend over, boys, here it comes!

Wow again. Feeling semi-stirred up her own self, Henryetta clicked open another *Femichismo!* article:

METHINKS THE LADDIE
DOTH PROTEST TOO MUCH
Rodent Chews Off Own Balls to Throw Feds Off Scent
By G.G. Carpenter, Editor-in-Chief

Under intense pressure from the Civil Rights Division of the U.S Department of Education to establish adequately strict policies and procedures for reining in sexual assaults against women on its

Cambridge, Massachusetts campus—either that or get shut off at the federal government ATM—the crumbling ivy-covered walls that hid Harvard's dungeons of depraved misogyny have finally been overrun by feminist revolutionaries. From the fetid bowels of the castle formerly harboring privileged white princes of perversion, however, comes a last desperate squeal for restoration of patriarchal power. By open letter published in the Boston Globe, twenty-eight moss-backed members of the notoriously reactionary Harvard Law School faculty whine that the university's new Office for Sexual and Gender-Based Dispute Resolution ("ODR") has adopted policies and procedures that violate basic constitutional principles of fairness and due process, in part because accused rapists need not be told who or what they did wrong, and are not entitled to a hearing.

Tough titty. Not a single woman signed the rotting parchment, hypocritically beginning with the words, "We the People," or voted for adoption of its content as a constitution. As for dealing with allegations of rape on campus,"Stop with the presumption of innocence already!" says Wendy Murphy, herself a law professor somewhere else. The rat pack of professors also complain about the set-up of an all-powerful Office of Gender and Sexual Dispute Resolution. So what? Even critics of ODR concede that if such a system had been in place and sternly employed at Duke University in 2006, the entire "Dukie" lacrosse team—along with the football squad, water boys and numerous "boosters"—would have been found guilty in that infamous case of injustice. And as Professor Murphy has effectively pointed out, ODRs are not empowered to assess death penalties, at least not yet, more's the pity!

Though few if any critics of the law professors' open letter have made much of their specifically self-serving complaint that the new policies and procedures are to apply <u>university-wide</u>, Femichismo! notes with suspicion that among the rogue's list of signatories to the *letter—and very likely the leader of the pack— is none other than Alan Dershowitz, an infamous, redheaded legal hack best known for defending the murder of a woman by a former campus jock named O.J. Simpson.*

OFF WITH HIS RED HEAD!

As Henryetta read another article—headlined **METHOUGHT SO!**—reporting that the Civil Rights Division of the Department of Education had later started a new investigation into sexual assaults of students at Harvard Law School "likely committed by Professor Dershowitz," Mr. Harold appeared beside her desk.

"Henryetta, I'm worried about Shat," he said, before setting down in a chair. "Over-supplied with Who-Struck-John, he's always been a little inclined to, well, having an original way with words that some might say is a little too colorful for a newspaper, especially a small town paper like the *Weekly Herald*. Even female law school students at Harvard are complaining about having to study rape law— the word 'violate' triggers too much trauma—which makes you wonder how they're gonna handle the subject of murder, or the tax code. Anyway, the Missus and her card-playing club of ladies are feeling vaporish about the OIC guards waggling their night sticks in his bean hole. I have never been one to compromise journalistic integrity, but…"

Henryetta waited as her boss went on fidgeting, like he always did when he had bad news to tell. He was likely going to cancel publication of Mr. Shat's **R***d Like Me** series, she reckoned, but…

"Anyway," he said, standing up straight, "I would sure appreciate it, Henryetta, if you would uncolor Shat's words some, and make 'em into toned down third-person installments under your own byline 'stead of runnin' 'em as Shat's anonymous reports. If Shat doesn't like it, well, he'll just have to lump it."

Land sakes alive! Promoted from footnote to byline for a story reported by the famous journalist, Shatner Lapp! Henryetta like to wet her pants.

EIGHTEEN

Standing on a makeshift platform inside OIC's large Rotunda, Ester Frigg—dressed in a standard Dean's pinstriped pantsuit, holding Martha Washington in one arm, a bullhorn in her other hand—surveyed her surroundings: On three tiers of balconies overlooking the large enclosed space, male correctees—freed from their cells for the special occasion—leaned over the balcony railings. Unnecessarily armed guards stood at unnecessarily strategic points on the edges of the expansive assembly hall. Before her, in the center of the ground level—a parade ground, so to speak—two hundred newly arrived young female correctees looked up to her with eyes wide in excited anticipation of the experience that lay ahead of them. The glorious day of OIC's blast-off into a co-educational future had arrived!

"Welcome, all co-eds—female and male—to the new Oklahoma Institute of Correctology," she shouted through the bullhorn. "Yes, you heard me correctly; at OIC women alone shall not be 'co' to the opposite gender, which in the past has implied we are in some way secondary to equally 'co' males." After pausing for applause that failed to materialize, Ester turned to specifically address the women: "All of you female co-eds are at least eighteen years of age; otherwise you would not have been eligible for enrollment. So you and your families have every Constitutional right to expect that under Title IX you will be provided with a warm, cozy and completely safe environment for your rehabilitation, complete with teddy bears in every bed. Indeed, I myself, as Dean, regard this as the highest, most sacred obligation of institutes of higher correction. Your comfort and 24/7 security is not up to you, not up to law enforcement authorities, nor up to anyone else but OIC and the Department of Education. To be plain and allay any fears you might have, I shall now briefly address what must be foremost on your minds."

"Doin' the Nasty!" someone shouted from above, and as a matter of fact, Ester—without use of the traumatizing R-word—intended to introduce the broad outlines of her policies, rules and procedures for dealing with inevitable gender-related misunderstandings on co-ed campuses that were most often of a sexual nature. "I know what that means!" she shouted upward. "And you, sir, shall soon find that I mean business when it comes to 'nasty' sex." Rude laughter rained down from the balconies.

"'Business? 'Tis pity, the boss lady is a whore!" came an answer to her statement. "Bring on the pussy, I've got a dollar in my pocket." More guffaws set Martha Washington to clawing the lapels of Ester's pantsuit. After handing her animal companion to Demoana, who stood beside the dais, rolling her eyes, Ester tidied her ball of hair and returned her attention to the assembly of well behaved women, none of whom were laughing. "You will find that I am not the kind of Dean who goes about with my head…"

"Stuck up your ass!" *Ha, ha, ha…*

"...in the sand. I realize quite well...

"It's too tight!" *Ha, ha, ha...*

"...that in close quarters, sexual 'hook-ups', as are bound to occur, are the private business of..."

"'Tis aint no pity, they're all in business!" *Ha, ha, ha, ha, ha...*

"...mutually <u>consenting</u> adults. But rest assured, I will not allow..."

"Beat me, whip me, Deanette. I'll never consent!" *Ha, ha, ha, ha, ha...*

"...the campus, uh, unwanted sex epidemic to spread inside the walls of OIC!"

Spread! Spread! Spread! the male correctees began to chant. *Spread 'em! Spread 'em! Spread 'em!...*

Ester, losing her patience, again put a hand to her unraveling bun of hair and looked the unruly mob of male co-eds in the whites of their eyes. "Your mess hall 'spread' shall consist of moldy bread and water for the remainder of the week!" she bellowed at the insufferable herd of braying hecklers, which quieted them sufficiently for her to continue.

"Now, as I was saying," she said, "I do not have my head in the <u>sand</u>; I know all about the birds and bees. Indeed, I have already authorized expansion of OIC facilities for 'conjugal-like' get-togethers, but not with spouses or anyone else from outside these walls. In the hook-up room and elsewhere on campus, my rules of proper conduct shall apply, to-wit: 'No' means 'No' at every step of your interactions with <u>them</u>," she announced to the women correctees, with a throw of her bun in the direction of the male heads circled above.

"Indeed, there was a time when this was clearly and mutually understood without need of the two-hundred pages of rules I shall be distributing," she said, taking an antique ladies fan from a breast pocket of her pantsuit. "Basic signals of engagement were as follows: Fan fast," she said, fanning fast, "meant you were available. Fan slow," she said, fanning slow, "meant you were committed to another. Fan with right hand in front of your face like this meant 'come on'; fan with left hand meant 'leave me alone'. And of course rapidly opening and shutting your fan like this meant…"

"You're hot!"

"…'kiss me'!"

Short fat Fanny to the rescue!
Short fat Fanny to the res-cue!
Short fat…

Ester again looked up at the male co-eds and this time shook a fist. "Fine, have your frat boy fun while you can," she shouted. "Starting at dawn tomorrow, I shall begin to personally drill you one by one on the rules that shall henceforth govern your conduct toward female co-eds!"

Short fat Fanny to the rescue!
Short fat Fanny to the res-cue!
Short fat…

Though rattled, Ester pressed on with the part of her prepared speech specifically directed at male correctees: "If your intended partner pulls down her top to reveal her ta-tas," she said, opening the fan in front of her own breasts, "but maintains this 'fan position'—metaphorically speaking—to invoke Rule Number One, you are to make no further advance, understood?!"

Short fat fanny is my heart's desire.
Short fat Fanny sets my soul on fire…

"If she signals 'all clear' by dropping her lowers, but only half closes her 'fan'… I am speaking metaphorically, you morons! I am simply illustrating that this signals her invocation of Rule

Number Two, at which point you are Constitutionally bound by Title IX to withdraw and zip up your trousers!"

Short fat Fanny is my heart's desire.

Short fat Fanny sets my _pecker_ *on fire! Ha, ha, ha, ha, ha, ha, ha…*

Ester fumed. "You frat boys may have heard certain online gossip spread by a jealous former colleague to the effect that I am a pushover," she shouted. "But if you do not learn and abide by my rules, you will find that I do indeed have the 'cojones'…"

"No, please, we believe you!"

"…to drop the hammer on each and every one of you. My rules of sexual conduct shall govern…"

I touched her on the thigh/ She said you're rather high/ Roll me over, lay me down, and do it again, they sang, each and every adolescent one of them, it seemed to Ester.

"Stop it! Stop it, I say! Or I shall shun you! I am serious: You shall be shunned!"

I touched her on the spot/ She said you're gettin' hot/ Roll me over, lay me down, and do it again/ Do it again/ Roll me ovvv-er, Roll me ovvv-er/ Roll me over, lay me down, and do it again/ Do it again!

Ester put a hand to her mouth and reached for Martha Washington, in horror that— at the very least—a retrograde verbal, and musical, strain of campus rape madness seemed to have already infected OIC!

NINETEEN

In the OIC visitors parking lot, trying to stuff an extra mini-bottle of Who-Struck-John into one of her jeans pockets, Henryetta puzzled over the sight of seven or eight unmarked school buses setting there. A prison was a strange place to take kids for a summer camp field trip, she thought. At the check-in desk for the conjugatin' room, she then got puzzled to find no one on duty, but...In the direction of a racket coming from somewhere, Henryetta walked down a long corridor—the noise getting louder as she went—and finally arrived at a sign identifying a big three or four-story space as a Rotunda. Land sakes alive! Dean Frigg stood on a box at one end, yelling into a bullhorn: "No means No! No means No! No means No!" In the center, a big bunch of gals in pink outfits and chains huddled like a flock of scared sheep. Up on steel walkways around the upper levels of the Rotunda, at least a hundred chained male inmates in orange outfits leaned over the railings and chanted back at the Dean: "No means Yes! Yes means..."

That was the crude chant she had read about in the *Femichismo!* archives; the one with words like the University of

Virginia "Rugby Road" song that had got a fraternity back at Yale put on probation, and the whole college put under federal investigation for its hostile environment that made women feel sexually harassed. Maybe what G.G. Carpenter said was true; maybe Dean Frigg had carried the germs of a campus rape culture from back east to OIC, Henryetta began to think, even before some of the male inmates started singing what sounded like one of those rude fraternity boy "drinking songs":

The women of OIC/ They fight for their chastity/ Fight everyone but we/ The men of Cell Block C!

"Stop it!" Dean Frigg hollered. "Words and lyrics offensive to women are no longer allowed here. Stop it this very minute, or else!" But her yelling seemed to cheer 'em' on to get rowdier.

A clique of inmates on the third level chanted: *Mary Ann McCarthy/ She wanted to get her clam shucked/ Mary Ann McCarthy/ She wanted to get her clam shucked/ And Mary Ann McCarthy..."*

Another group on the second level chimed in: *Mary fell into a bed of oysters/ Mary fell into a bed of oysters/ Mary fell into a bed of oysters/ And Mary got her clam shucked."*

"Stop it! Stop it, I say!"

Then the unruliest bunches, who must have been members of the rival gangs Leon seemed to have took for "frats," got to singing back and forth at each other:

If we catch a an Aryan Brother inside these prison walls/ We'll take him to the Rec Hall and amputate his balls!

If a Bohica yells for mercy, this is what we'll do/ We'll stuff his ass with broken glass and seal it up with glue!

"Cease and desist! I say, cease and desist from this sexual harassment!" the Dean insisted. Lights blinked on and off. An odor of fried bacon blew in through air conditioning ducts. A siren blared. Guards rushed onto the steel walkways and started pushing the male inmates, still singing, into their cells.

Drinkin' beer in O'Riley's bar/ tellin' tales of blood and slaughter/ Thoughts kept runnin' through my mind/ thought I'd shag O'Riley's daughter? Diddly-aye-a/ Diddly-aye-o/ Diddly-aye for one-ball Riley/ Rub-a-dub-dub, shag all!

Screw 'em all, screw 'em all/ Screw the wide and the short and the tall…

After the ruckus settled down, "That unfortunate display of incorrectness was most regrettable," Dean Frigg bellowed at the new female inmates, "but let's not let it spoil your first day at OIC. I assure you that with power vested in me by Title IX, I shall make this institute a safe and comfortable collegiate environment for your rehabilitation. And to further enhance your experience here, my assistant, Demoana, seated to my right, has enrollment forms for a host of women-only extracurricular activities. For those of you interested in wholesome athletics, Coach Downs, to my left, is organizing a number of women's sports teams. Now, let's all enjoy our koolade and cookies, as we begin to get acquainted with one another."

Headed toward the Dean to ask a few questions, Henryetta got caught by the eye of a good looking young black fella, smiling at her. She detoured in his direction. Maybe she did have an itch for bad boys, she reckoned, as she got up close to him. He was an inmate alright, dressed in a regular orange outfit, though he was not in chains like the others, and seemed to have free run of the Rotunda. She introduced herself. He stuck out a hand. "How do you do," he said. "My name is Buddy Brown." Henryetta had never before got such a polite greeting from a male of any age or status. "I'm a trusty," he explained, "and a blue-chip wideout on the football team, which means I run fast and catch passes."

"What are you in for?" she asked, hoping he wasn't gonna

turn out to be a rapist or somethin'. "And more to the point, how long 'til they let you out?"

"I'm doing time for cutting up," he said, semi-hanging down his head. Uh oh, guys who carried around sharp knives, like Leon used to do, had always made her semi-uneasy. "Yeah, pranks and dirty tricks in class: spitballs, whoopee cushions in teachers' chairs, pulling at girls' pigtails; I've got a rap sheet as long as my arm."

Huh, Henryetta began to worry that Buddy Brown, her first chance at any extracurricular romantic activity since Gus was a pup, must be gay; like Gaylord's football teammate and significant other, Billy Ray Williams, who also played wideout. And wouldn't you know it, Buddy Brown went on to say that his ambition was to someday play for the Dallas Cowboys, just like Billy Ray, and Gaylord. He said that for him and a lot of the newer inmates, playing for the OIC Wild Bunch was a stop on a "career path" made necessary by colleges gettin' out of the pigskin business.

"And my parents thought I was getting too distracted by girlfriends, so my father—he's the Mayor of Tulsa—pulled some strings and got me into OIC." That was a relief to Henryetta, the part about him being prone to distractions from girlfriends. "I hope to graduate early, in a year or two, after I've made a name for myself on the field," he said, "which reminds me: I'm running late for my daily extra workout. See you around campus, Henryetta."

Reminded that she her own self should be working on her own career path, Henryetta went over to Dean Frigg. "I'm Henryetta," she said, to re-introduce herself, "spelled with a y where an i should've been put 'cause my mother, Wynona Sue, named me for the little ol' town I was born in."

"Cry me a river," said the Dean, waving a hand in front of her face, maybe to clear away bacon odor still in the air. "My mother married a man named Frigg, solely for the purpose of providing her 'illegitimate' daughter with a 'proper' name."

When Henryetta then informed Ms. Frigg she was a correspondent for *Femichismo!*, the Dean's eyes narrowed. When she mentioned that her editor was G.G. Carpenter, they closed almost tight shut. "Ms. G.G. tells me you two were college roommates, known around Wellesley campus as a walrus and a carpenter."

Dean Frigg went to grinding her teeth. "I was told you were a correspondent for *The New York Times*, not for that... that anarchist online gossip page," she said. And with that, the "walrus" turned on a heel and waddled away.

Henryetta hurried along beside her and persisted: "Ms. Carpenter worries that as a neo-Victorian sort of Dean you might find the weeds too deep down here for you to lead OIC's change-over to co-education. So I was wonderin' about possible spread of the campus rape epidemic from Harvard down here to..."

Uh oh. Ms. Frigg stopped herself, and with a stone cold stare brought Henryetta also to a halt. "For your information, Ms. What's-Your-Name, the 'Walrus' and the 'Carpenter' are the fictional title characters of an amusing Lewis Carroll poem from *Alice's Adventures in Wonderland*," she said, chilly as a stepmother's smile, "in which the two of them take a troop of oysters for a gambol along a shoreline; and talk nonsense. If you bothered to read the poem and checked with people who knew Ms. Carpenter and me during our time at Wellesley College—from which I graduated *Magna Cum Laude* and my 'colleague', a boy- crazy slut, dropped out—you would find that the 'Walrus' led the beach escapade <u>and</u> the feminist cause at Wellesley, while the 'Carpenter' simply tagged along for awhile and made stupid remarks. Neither you nor your 'editor' need fear sexual assault on these premises. I am quite up to thwarting any such occurrence here at the Oklahoma Institute of Correctology, of which I am in total control. So there!"

As more of that "frat boy" singing came from the cells around the Rotunda, Henryetta reckoned that Dean Frigg had already done a lot to make OIC seem like one of those eastern colleges showed in old movies. Whether she was up to the job of overseeing switch of the "college" to co-ed, well...*Princeton's run by Wellesley/ Wellesley's run by Yale/ Yale is run by Vassar/ and Vassar's run by tail/ Harvard's run by stiff pricks/ the kind you raise by hand/ But OIC is run by us sons of bitches/ the baddest in the land!* ...Henryetta had her doubts.

TWENTY

Lying on the upper bunk of his two-man cell, looking up at a blank patch of ceiling, Leon misted up a little. He'd taken down the magazine center-spread with a cut-out of Henryetta's high school yearbook picture stuck on a bathing beauty's face. Having her up there on top of him, naked, just didn't seem right no more. And she didn't look like that no more neither. There was something about Henryetta now—he couldn't put his finger on it—that had sorta changed. She was still pretty though, and he missed her. With the correctology institute on lock-down since the ruckus in the Rotunda to welcome split-tails, he had not been able to keep a date with her in the conjugatin' room. His new cellmate, Buddy Brown—who was one of OIC's trusted trustys—had took Mr. Sheep Dog's toilet paper messages to her in his place. Buddy had volunteered to do that for him, and since no one else was willing to be his cellie, Buddy had also volunteered to move in and help him with his homework.

He had learned a lot about Reconstructed American Herstory in Miz Frigg's class. For instance, though he had already heard about a War on Women, from watching the *Alice in Wonderland* cartoon movie dozens of times, he'd thought it was a war on women by other women; and that the White Queen and her army had already beat the Red Queen to end the war. And while he had also heard of the first man <u>on</u> the moon and the man <u>in</u> the moon, he'd never known that meant the moon—female and named 'Luna'—had got raped by an astronaut. For another thing: Someone named George Washington wasn't no hero to be bragged on for not telling a lie; he was an over-privileged white brat to be shat on for chopping down a tree in the first place. There was gonna be a big test in writing tomorrow. Leon was nervous about it, and...

Buddy walked in with a piece of paper in his hand. "Okay, Leon, it's time to study up on Reconstructed American Herstory," he said, before flopping onto the lower bunk. "I happened to run across a written copy of the test question in a locked drawer. It's a tricky one about George Washington."

"Oh yeah, I remember you saying he was Dean Frigg's husband, and to make a note."

"No, you're confusing Dean Frigg with Martha Washington, who is a cat."

"George Washington <u>married</u> a cat?"

"Who's to say. The test question is: 'Why is George Washington <u>correctly</u> known as father of our bastard country? Because (a) he was unusually tall, (b) he was a military leader, (c) he was our first President, (d) he was a surveyor, (e) none of the above, or (f) all of the above?'"

"Dang! That is tricky. <u>Was</u> George Washington our real father, or a stepdaddy?"

"He's known as our father for all the reasons listed (a) through (d), but according to Dean Frigg he is <u>correctly</u> known as daddy only because he was a surveyor."

"Oh yeah, I remember her gettin all het up about that, but… What's a 'surveyor'?"

"The U.S. of A. was unsettled wilderness back in the day, and George Washington's first job was to take one of those telescope gizmos—that Dean Frigg called his 'penis'—put it up to his eye…"

"Wow! How tall was he?"

"He used the gizmo to rape the virgin bush of Mother Nature."

"That mf'ing S.O.B.! Then they went and put up that big monument of his sharp-pointed penis anyway, and named that state after him; the one called…Georgia?"

"Don' think about it too much, Leon; just put a circle around (d)."

"Raped Mother Nature; why would any man do such a thing?"

"Well, all real men scarf a ho now and then, right? I know I have, lots of times."

Scarf? Leon admitted that he didn't know what the word meant. Buddy said the cool guys at his Tulsa high school bragged about "scarfing" girls, one after the other. Then, after a long pause, Buddy admitted he didn't know exactly what they were talking about. In the dim light of the cell, sort of like Boy Scouts beside a campfire, Leon—who had never been a Boy Scout and never had a real buddy like Buddy—felt it was safe to confess that his experience with the opposite sex was limited to dry humping female farm animals. He had never even danced with a real girl.

"What?!" Buddy sprang out of the lower bunk and began to pace. "Dang it, Leon, you're two or three years older and have been around. I figured you for an experienced ass man who could coach me on how to get in the pants of a certain little ho, who's got the hots for me. Heck, that's why I moved in here to help you with homework."

"Hey, man, I was just funnin'," said Leon, trying to regain his 'man card', "but let me give you some advice: Don't go tellin' other dudes about hot little hos or they might just snatch the snatch for theirselves, know what I mean?"

"Yeah, well, it was you your own self who let me in on that little blue-eyed bitch with the black Afro…"

Black Afro? <u>That</u> was the different thing about Henryetta, Leon realized, with a sudden churn in his stomach; she had re-done her hair!

"…and now she is frothin' for my bod. So I guess the joke's on you, dude."

Leon felt his heart break.

Buddy walked out of the cell, probably to go find a new bunkmate, Leon imagined. That was the last straw that also broke his back. Since giving up *Stud* horse pills, he had already lost weight and most of his built-up muscles. Realizing he was never gonna be a football hero like Gaylord Goodhart, he had also lost interest in getting his eligibility back to play blocking dummy. Now his girlfriend, Henryetta, was frothin' for another guy; and just as hurtful, he had lost his best, and only, buddy.

To take his mind off the pain, Leon rolled over onto his belly and opened a book. It wasn't even wrote down in American a-b-c letters; he couldn't understand a word of it; but Miz Frigg had said that if he studied the book, called *The Koran*—and became an Islamian—he might be able to get into a Harvard Law School back east after she'd finished with him at OIC. He had already sent in an application to a Professor Dershowitz, who…

BALLS

Buddy came back with a can of beer in each one of his hands, but kept both to hisself; re-flopped onto the lower bunk; and said nothin'. It stayed real quiet between them for a long while.

"I haven't been around nowhere in my whole life, Buddy," said Leon, to break the awkward silence between them. "But I have known Henryetta since we were kids in grade school back in the little ol' hometown that she's named for—spelled with a y where an i should have been put. She's not like other girls; she's special; she's the best one ever. And I can tell you from my own experience: She is not gonna cotton to you if you change from the polite manners that have already got her frothin'. If you just keep on treating her like a cheerleader, Buddy, you'll likely get in her pants and find out what 'scarfing' means."

That said, Leon rolled over onto his side to face a blank wall, and closed his watery eyes.

TWENTY-ONE

Henryetta, frustrated as a honeymooner with a bad case of poison ivy, re-read the e-mail she had just got from G.G. Carpenter at *Femichismo!*

Re: your submission, "Powerful Oklahoma Woman Razes Helen," REJECTED! This <u>Mrs.</u> Rutledge you praise as "<u>macho</u>woman" should have used her husband's bulldozer to "e-raze" him, not the house of his girlfriend, "Helen," for crying out loud. The weeny-<u>wife</u>, "Katie," obviously will do anything to hold onto the "no-account" man who makes her tail wag. The husband, "Larry," is the villain. Find a story about a "macho<u>male</u>," cut off his "Rocky Mountain oysters" with a sharp story slant and roast them to a crisp! Otherwise, H.E., I am afraid you may have to find another outlet for your brand of journalism, such as Woman's Home Companion, if patriarchal poppycock is still peddled under that silly brand.

Dang it! Henryetta, like she should have done at G.G. Carpenter's first mention of the word, opened her computer dictionary, entered *p–a–t–r–i–a–r–c–h*—by mistake typed a y where an al should have been put—and came up with **pat*tri*arch*y:** *a system of society or government in which men hold* *the power and women are largely excluded from it.* Hmm. Henryetta went to the *NewsOK* website in search of local or state news items about powerful women and mean men that she could put a sharp slant to. She found **Wellesley Women Demand Campus Stalker Begone,** but no, the "stalker" traumatizing the college women was only a statue of a man in underwear. She found **Frat Boys Seek Sex With 4 our of 5 Women on Campus,** but nope, that didn't happen in Oklahoma neither. She then came across **"Power Crazed" Women in High Office Get Right-Wing Senator's Goat,** which sounded semi-promising.

Henryetta read that a State Senator was trying to impeach Lieutenant Governor O'Fallon for putting a "female lunatic from out of state" in total charge of the Oklahoma Institute of Correctology. Hmm. After jotting some notes from the article, Henryetta started typing a re-slanted piece of aggregated news for *Femichismo!*

A right-wing Oklahoma State Senator, Charles B. Lutz, semi-famous statewide for wanting a law for ten commandments to be tattooed on the rear ends of all female newborns, is now attacking two grown-up women for being powerful. "The Lieutenant Governor (Pricilla "Prissy" O'Fallon) and that other bitch down at OIC (Dean Ester Frigg) have put this year's football season in danger," said the wacky political patriarch. "The whole team is on lock-down because that new Warden from back east—who must think she's Hillary Clinton and wants to turn my alma mater into an all-girl Wellesley College—thought a little funnin' by the boys threatened an outbreak of rape, which I call horse feathers." According to the Senator's petition to the Supreme Court, Ms. O'Fallon and Ms. Frigg, by keeping gals and guys in separate but unequal facilities, have failed to sexually integrate OIC as required by the U.S. Constitution; and are also guilty of unconstitutional sexism by not adding a single woman to Death Row during Dean Frigg's first weeks on the job. But as previously reported by Femichismo! (here), no woman ever signed the rotten parchment beginning "We the People."

It is Senator Lutz his own self who ought to have his gonads roasted on Mama Megawatt's lap, for lying about there being no danger of the rape epidemic spreading into the Oklahoma Institute of Correctology. According to reliable sources embedded inside the walls of OIC, rape is already going on every day and night in a certain area of the institute. Maybe Senator Lutz ought to go on down there to see for hisself.

BOHICA!

After some polishing of her piece, Henryetta sent it to *Femichismo!*, then leaned back in her chair to wait on G.G. Carpenter to reply. Hitting back at patriarchy had made her feel semi-giddy, she realized, almost like puffing on a marijuana cigarette at a party. Maybe she would dig up more to say about that no-account Senator Lutz and get him impeached, she began to think. Maybe she had finally caught on to the kind of journalism angle G.G. Carpenter wanted, and would now start to get paid for…Henryetta answered her buzzing eye-phone.

"G.G. here, we need to talk, H.E." Uh oh, here it came, Henryetta thought, but…"My Goddess, you've got a source inside Ester's institute? Is she a rape victim herself, I hope?"

"Well, the source is actually a 'he' and 'Sheep Dog' is not really a 'victim' of the reliable sort…"

"SHE IS A VICTIM! enough said," her boss shouted. "My Goddess, are you one of those so-called fact sticklers who refuse to give rapists their Constitutional presumption of guilt?! Do you buy into the right-wing bullshit that women make false claims of a rape epidemic on campus?"

"No, it's just that…Didn't you read what I wrote about that

no-account politician in the state senate who…"

"Rejected! The senator is an asshole, of course, but a secondary target in our fight against patriarchy. The primary enemy… Open your eyes, H.E. Men created the oppressive patriarchal culture of western civilization, true; their day of reckoning will come. But our immediate <u>arch</u> enemy, well…Think of us, the no-more-bullshit radical feministas, as Sunni Wahhabis. Think of Ester Frigg and her eely cohorts as Shiites. We are engaged in an ideological civil war that must be won by us, the Wahhabis, in order to ultimately bring about the downfall of western mankind."

Wow! Henryetta had never thought of herself as Wahhabi or Shiite, and wasn't sure she wanted to ever get into a war against <u>all</u> men. In fact, since meeting Buddy Brown down at OIC, she had been scheming how to get him to come inside the conjugatin' room when he brought toilet paper pages from Mr. Shat.

"Don't worry, H.E. It's your lead, you'll get a byline for the big story," said her *Femichismo!* editor. "But you're young, not simple minded exactly, but a little naive and…What's your contact's name? I need to be put in direct touch: To get past him and scoop the straight poop from the victim, 'Sheep Dog'."

"Uh, this particular rape story has a semi-different angle from the usual sharp *Femichismo!* one," said Henryetta.

"No problem. I'll twist her arm and angle to suit, once I dispose of this male…Let me guess: He's an OIC 'counselor' and has told the victim to tell her story to no one else, right? Is he trying to sell the 'Sheep Dog's' tale? No way, I want her first-person account unsullied by his dirty hands. What's the son of a bitch's name?"

"Well, uh, he goes by the name of 'Jamus Murphy' inside OIC, but actually, Ms. Carpenter, 'Sheep Dog' is…"

"Say no more on the phone," G.G. Carpenter commanded. "I will get myself down there as soon as possible. I want direct personal contact with Mr. Murphy to discuss financial terms for access to the victim. Some might call the offer I make to him a threat of blackmail, but that would be impossible, wouldn't it? I know nothing about the man to expose, other than he is a scum-sucking male, right?"

Oops, Henryetta had got her toe stuck deeper in the crack between two of her bosses. "For you your own self to get in, uh, direct personal contact with Mr. Murphy might be a problem," said Henryetta. "You'd better bring along a pack of condoms."

"Condoms? Oh, I see," said the quick-thinking, fast-talking *Femichismo!* editor. "My apologies, H.E. I've underestimated you and your commitment to our cause."

The phone clicked off, and Henryetta set to worrying: Had she semi-accidentally betrayed Mr. Shat? He wouldn't have to send out any toilet paper messages to G.G. Carpenter in reply to hers, but how would he react to her even getting in semi-direct contact with him by way of his Death Row bean hole?

TWENTY-TWO

∧∧∧∧∧∧∧∧∧∧
∧∧∧∧∧∧∧∧∧∧
∧∧∧∧∧∧∧∧∧∧

Lying on his concrete Cadillac, his head rested comfortably on a fluffy pillow, Shat took a a hearty swig from a half-pint bottle of *Wild Turkey*, then lit a cigar. With the help of a resourceful buddy, the mule, Leon, had proved to be a useful idiot with remarkable capacity to deliver the goods. Having not lived so well for the past few years, Shat had begun to entertain thoughts of an extended stay at Oklahoma's Graybar Hotel. There was much work to be done in the midst of OIC's takeover by the damned feministas. They, those bitches, more so than the guards and frat boys on campus, were the oppressed black man's arch enemies. They had to be stopped from stealing thunder from the African-American civil rights struggle. A first-hand account of their radical feminist revolution from inside the walls would add a zesty angle to his age-old morality tale, along with newsworthiness and publicity value. With a copy of the feminista propaganda magazine *Douche*—recently shoved into his cell—for use as an easel, so to speak, Shat took ball point pen in hand, and on a fresh roll of toilet paper began to sketch an outline for another installment of **R***d Like Me**:

Tap, Tap, Tap. Though Death Row is eerily devoid of the usual mindless yelling and screaming of its condemned men, the natives are restless tonight. Messages being transmitted in code through the AC ducts warn of danger afoot. Tap, Tap, Tap. Yes, a brigade of feminista shock troops have established a beachhead inside the walls of this institute of correctology that I dare not name. According to reports by frightened guards, almost all male inmates are on 'round the clock lock-down. And here we sit, the desperate men of Cell Block D, trapped in our cells, unarmed and defenseless. Tap, Tap, Tap. Fear among we oppressed African-American males is palpable, and why shouldn't it be. Bros have been dragged to Yellow Mama with increased frequency since appointment of a bull dyke—known as Short Fat Fanny—to be Warden. The odor of bacon is now thick as hair spray I recently encountered in a small town whore house. Oh yeah, she—the virtual Whore of Babylon by all accounts—is leader of a feminist conspiracy to cook our black gooses. Tap, Tap, Tap.

And her band of she-devils seem to have formed an unholy alliance of at least temporary convenience with frat boys in other cell blocks. Snatches of riotous singing and laughing from their drunken debauch of last week drifted down to Death Row like propaganda leaflets aimed at destroying our morale and will to resist their advance:

"...catch a...Brother...inside the walls/ take him to...and amputate his balls!"

"...yells for mercy...what we'll do/ stuff his ass... and seal it up with glue!"

"...screw 'em... screw 'em all/...screw the wide and the short and the tall!"

"...run by stiff pricks...raised by hand/ but OIC is run by ... bitches..."

The effect was terrifying, and now as we cower in our cells, afraid to sleep lest the feminist she-devils make a nighttime sneak attack and suck us dry of testosterone.

Tap! Tap! Tap! Tap! Tap! Tap! Tap! Tap!

Realizing that actual tapping had come, not by way of Death Row's jungle telegraph, but from the steel door of his cell, Shat leapt from his Cadillac. His half-full half-pint bottle of whiskey shattered on the concrete floor. In panic, he pressed his back against a wall, as the door inched open!

"Have you, by any chance, seen Martha Washington?"

Great balls afire! In the doorway, stalking him like a…It had to be the Great Whore of Babylon herself, come to suck the life out of his doodads!

"She's Persian," said the monstrous bull dyke, adorned with a large coughed-up ball of cat hair on her head. "Short, heavy-boned legs," she said, "stout body, large expressive eyes; long hair the color of mine, but of course not up in a bun. I think of us as sisters. She spent hours earlier today, sharpening her claws," said the beast, with a glance at her own long, sharp fingernails, "so I fear she is, to put it delicately, 'on the prowl'."

"No, please, no," Shat said, as the monstrous bull dyke sprawled onto his Cadillac and curled up like a giant cat. He had to catch himself from falling to the floor to lap up the spilled bourbon mixed with shards of glass. Earlier, he had detected an odor of burning hair, he now recalled, but dared not speak of it.

"I do not approve of tobacco usage," she said, with a look toward the dead stogie on the concrete cot beside her; "nor drinking," she added. "On the other hand," she purred, pulling the knees of her short, strong-boned legs up to her ample chest to curl tighter and cozier into a ball, "all work and no play would make you a dull boy, Mr, uh…"

"Shatner Lapp," he blurted. "I mean…"

"I am Dean Frigg, but I hope you will someday come to

'know' me as 'Ester'."

"…Sheep Dog Murphy is my real name. I'm a new dull boy from New Hampshire."

"My word, I too hail from the Granite State. Heretofore, I've been more of a cat person than dog fancier, but…I have a feeling you may be a tomcat in sheep dog disguise, Mr. Murphy. Tee, hee. What's your sign? Not a Leo, I hope; not a ferocious, snarling lion who might 'eat me up'. Tee, hee."

As the abominable feline creature from hell continued to mew in an obscenely flirtatious vein, Shat began to feel like one of the little oysters in that well known Lewis Carroll poem from *Alice's Adventures in Wonderland*; himself about to be eaten up by a ravenous walrus. He wanted to cry, "RAPE!" But given Short Fat Fanny's position of absolute authority over him, he didn't dare overtly resist her advances.

"I'm a cold blooded murderer," he said, but she didn't flinch. "Oh yeah, I am not really a sheepish dog, I am a <u>mad</u> <u>dog</u> killer, completely deserving of electrocution, which I expect to happen any day now. So I have nothing to lose and am likely to kill again if I get the chance. Might as well hang for an old goat as for a lamb, right? See what I'm sayin'? Maybe you should go look for…"

"I didn't know 'ewe' cared," she replied, batting her large unexpressive muddy eyes, and giggling at her little play on words. "Don't be so hard on yourself, Mr. Murphy, and do not overly worry. As long as I am Dean of OIC—and I do expect to have lifetime tenure here—no one in my 'TLC' on this so-called 'Death Row' shall…" She paused to adjust her bulbous ta-tas. "Arghh!" he blurted, as she then straightened one short heavy-boned leg to strike a grotesque oldtime bathing beauty pose.

"Though of course, in light of new information recently provided to me, I am torn," she continued in a coquettish tone. "While heretofore I have been an ardent opponent of the death penalty—indeed I wrote my doctoral dissertation on the futility of that cruel and unusual means of motivating would-be miscreants to toe the line—I am also ardently committed to saving mankind from climate change. I saw Al Gore's movie six times, and cried at his every lip movement. If promotion of wind power is necessary to proving we do not need those dirty old fossil fuels for such things as electrocution, well, I am sure you agree: Going along with a death penalty or two would be a small price to pay."

Shat understood all to well where the horny bitch was coming from. Through the years, he'd had his way with many a spicy professional subordinate by use of similar subtle hints. Now, it was payback time, on Death Row!

"Not to overly worry," she said again. "As you get to know me better, as 'Ester', you will find that I, like Martha Washington, have a sweet and gentle nature: playful but never demanding; able to easily adapt to any circumstance, if given love and reassurance; tremendously responsive and a constant source of joy and delight; pleasurable as an unexpected sunbeam; my companionship close and enduring."

She belched.

"Arghh!"

"And anyway, they tell me this new and improved 'Mama Megawatt' will zap with voltage sufficient to instantly turn a live elephant into a piece of charcoal sculpture," she said, rising from the Cadillac with large, round eyes, expressive of lubricious desire for hobble-de-gee. "So I feel quite sure that, say, a cuddly 'Sheep Dog', wouldn't know what hit him."

"Did you say Martha Washington was a <u>cat</u>?" said Shat, backing toward the cell door. "Because now that I think of it, I recall hearing Raw Dawg calling 'pussy, pussy, pussy' through the bean hole of his cell down at the end of the corridor, next door to Mama's room." That ruination of "the mood" stopped her advance. "Another time perhaps," she said, before bolting out of his cave and locking the door behind her.

Up on the lips of the lidless crapper, with ballpoint pen in hand, Shat began to frantically tap on the A/C grill.

Tap, Tap, Tap.

Having been only a baldfaced white boy at the Lawrenceville School long ago, he had not mastered the jungle telegraph code used by oppressed African-American men in prison.

Tap, Tap, Tap.

So he had not literally understood the messages sent by other Death Row inmates via the rusted sheet metal vine

Tap, Tap, Tap.

He had intuitively interpreted the signals' meaning, though not entirely sure the taps were not random rattles in the antiquated AC system.

Tap, Tap, Tap.

Equally unsure that his own tap, tap, taps would be heard and intuitively translated by others as cries of "Rape! Rape! Rape!' Shat continued to pound the grille with the ballpoint pen:

Tap, Tap, Tap, Tap, Tap, Tap, Tap, Tap, Tap, Tap, Tap, Tap... For God's sake, TAP! TAP! TAP!

TWENTY-THREE

Sensing Mr. Harold hovering over her from behind, Henryetta looked up from reading Mr. Shat's account of getting a "chilling fan card" and two-hundred rules for sex from Dean Frigg. Uh oh, her boss held a sheet of lined yellow paper with handwriting in pencil on it; no doubt an original piece of work for one of his front page editorials: "This one is a corker that will make folks sit up and take notice of what's going on," her boss said, as usual, before heading out the door. Henryetta set to word processing the piece of work:

From Where I Sit…………………An Editorial By Harold Mixon
BALLSHEVIK REVOLUTION OF 2015

One hundred years ago, Marxist revolutionaries led a civil war against the Tsarist regime in Russia. This comes to mind because, similarly, there is a feminist revolutionary movement on the march in the United States. The angry female uprising to overthrow so-called patriarchy—waged most visibly by propaganda—appears to be centered on college campuses throughout the country. And I fear that what might be called the "Ballsheviks," those radical feminists who seek to empower women by emasculating males, have gained the upper hand. Their anthem—"Hide your wife, hide your kids. Hide your wife, hide your kids"—proclaims that frat boys and jocks are "snatchin' up women" and "rapin' everybody out here". That there is a rape epidemic afoot on college campuses requiring extreme counter-measures akin to martial law is scarcely subject to question in the public mind, but not in mine.

In the words of Mark Twain, let's first review a couple of the "lies, damned lies, and statistics" of radical feminist propaganda…

Mr. Harold went on to say in pencil some things that had been buzzing inside Henryetta's own head—that the one-out-of-five college gals gettin' sexually assaulted statistic was likely more made up than correctly added up, for instance—and he took a whole different view than G.G. Carpenter of the campus rape epidemic spreading from Duke University to the University of Virginia. *For anyone who doubts we are confronted by a militant, ideological cult, consider these fairly typical feminist reactions to the discredited Rolling Stone piece,* **A Rape on Campus: A Brutal Assault and Struggle for Justice at UVA:**

"So what if this instance was more fictional than fact and didn't actually happen," said online magazine editor, Katie Racine in The Huffington Post. "This story (told by Rolling Stone) was a shock and awe campaign." Etcetera, etcetera.

Then mild mannered Mr. Harold went to ranting about a new statute in California and new procedures and rules to handle accusations of sexual assault at Harvard that a bunch of law professors had criticized as not fair, starkly one-sided and stacked against boys. *In a rebuttal of laughable, no doubt unintended satire worthy of the comedic Harvard Lampoon, editors of Harvard's student newspaper, the Crimson, opined that the law professors' concerns amounted to much ado about nothing, while conceding that "in rare cases of false accusation, it would be horrible to see a student unable to defend himself or herself for lack of financial means that would privilege one student over another."* Mr. Harold thanked God that an Equal Rights Amendment to the United States Constitution didn't get ratified back in the 1970s, and wrote that again, for some reason, "the Russian Revolution, Moscow show trials and Siberian exile" came to his mind…*As of 1915, Marxist opposition to the Tsarist regime was split into two main factions…*

Through the *Weekly Herald*'s storefront window, Henryetta saw that a big, boxy Ryder rental truck had pulled up and parked across the street. A tall gal wearing a white pantsuit got out of the truck and marched toward the office. When she came through the door, Henryetta saw that the gal semi-resembled what Lesley Stahl, the famous TV newswoman, must have looked like in her semi-younger days; except that this one's blonde hair was done in a manly butch cut. Yep, the visitor with a Senior Campfire Girls pink headband running across her forehead had to be G.G. Carpenter, alright and… "G.G. Carpenter," she confirmed, in a tone chilly as a pawnbroker's smile, "here to see H.E. Hebert, on important business." Henryetta stood up, and in her own cool manner told Ms. Carpenter who she was, without mention of her mother, Wynona Sue, or how she got to be named "H.E."

"You <u>are</u> young, and short," said the *Femichismo!* Editor-in-Chief, "but I like your retro do, H.E. On you, still has something of a radical vibe to it."

In no mood for girly chit-chat about hair, Henryetta got right down to what had been chafing her: "You haven't answered my e-mails and eye-phone calls," she said. "I my own self have been waiting for ten whole days to tell about important business."

"Sorry, thought I copied you: We've gone to the mattresses, H.E. Had to shut down electronic communications for security.

But tell me, what's happened? Has that little 'tea pot', short and stout, already cried out …"

"Tea pot? What in tarnation…?"

"I refer to Ester Frigg, of course, by one of her college nicknames, you might say. What's happened at OIC? Has the pressure gotten to Ester? Is OIC already boiling over?"

Henryetta stomped a foot. "I'm not gonna say no more about Dean Frigg and OIC. In fact…Well, first I want you to know, Ms. Carpenter, that I my own self have done some journalistic checking of facts . . "

"Good for you."

"…and a lot of the stories in the *Femichismo!* archives — that you your own self wrote — are wrong as rumors of roosters layin' eggs on rooftops."

"Such as?" the Editor-in-Chief answered, putting both hands on her narrowish hips.

"Such as that article — headlined **DUKE DEVILS DEBASE DEB** — about those college lacrosse team players. They didn't rape that black gal back in 2006, like you said they did. And I didn't find no retraction or correction in *Femichismo!* archives."

G.G. Carpenter spread her arms up in the air. "So what?" she said. "*The New York Times* reported, in so many words — almost six thousand in a single piece, as a matter of fact — that the 'black gal' had, at the very least, a credible story that should have gone to a jury. The *Times* is the world's official newspaper of record, you know, and its editors have not seen fit to make any correction to its scathing indictment of those demonic college jocks at Duke. To the contrary, in a related story about the black deb being found guilty of murdering a no doubt abusive boyfriend just a few years ago, the *Times* still referred to her as the 'victim' in the lacrosse team case. The Duke faculty also stands firm in its conviction that something happened that night, and that those hell raising jocks should pay the ultimate price for…"

"The Attorney General of the State of North Carolina took over the investigation," Henryetta argued. "He found out those rowdy college boys were not only <u>not guilty</u>; he officially declared they were downright <u>innocent</u>! The District Attorney who tried to put 'em in jail was the guilty one who got his lawyer license took from him for what <u>he</u> did! And then, earlier this very year you wrote…"

"You're missing the point, H.E. The Duke lacrosse story told a bigger truth transcending the bare facts…"

"Is that the same as makin' up bare facts like that *Rolling Stone* reporter did to tell a big truth about frat boys rapin' a gal at the University of Virginia? You your own self repeated the story on the *Femichismo!* main page—and said its moral was 'to die for'—like you were glad more wood had been piled on the news bonfire about a campus rape epidemic. It was same as the Duke story—'cept for mention of a beer bottle 'stead of a broomstick—'chapter and verse of a same old story'—you said, like it had been copied down from *Femichismo!* or somethin'."

"The *Rolling Stone* story was 'to die for' because it spoke powerful truth to power," said G.G. Carpenter, still as cool as Henryetta was hot. "The reporter, Ms. Ederly, told a riveting morality tale. <u>Something</u> happened in that despicable frat house. And there are similar makings for such a narrative right here in your home state, virtually sitting in our lap. You could be credited with contribution to a feminist Bullitzer Prize winner, H.E. But if you are going to be so picky, picky, picky…"

"And I also looked at that disgusting video you gave a *Femichismo!* 'Golden Dildo Prize' to," said Henryetta, lathered up and not to be put off— *F-BOMBS FOR FEMINISM: Potty-Mouthed Princesses Use Bad Word for Good Cause*—which about made me gag at the sight of little girls in pink dresses, spouting hateful words against boys not really of a childish "potty" kind and a lot uglier than just F-bombs! 'We're not princesses in distress, stop telling us how to dress,' they chant. 'Teach mf'ers not to f...ing rape.' That mother at the end—wearing a tee-shirt with THIS IS WHAT A FEMINIST LOOKS LIKE wrote on it—should be sent to prison."

"Are little princesses saying off-color words more shocking than the fact that one out of five college girls are sexually assaulted on campuses?" G.G. Carpenter answered. "And you may not have noted that the video producer is donating a portion of proceeds from the mom's tee-shirt sales to a worthy cause.

"I think it's all just propaganda for a feminist revolution," said Henryetta, quoting Mr. Harold. "I think you your own self must be a...a Ballshevik!"

"'Ballshevik', that's good, H.E. You have a way with words. But if you're gong to be so picky, picky, picky, I'm afraid I may have to consider..."

"Don't bother doin' any considering," said Henryetta, "I quit. And if you want to know the powerful truth about 'Sheep Dog'..."

"Oh, I <u>will</u> know her story, and will waterboard the poor dear if that's what it takes to get her to go on record," said G.G. Carpenter, with a look in her pretty blue eyes that could've iced down a case of beer. "Mr. Murphy will give up 'Sheep Dog' to us, if it takes a case of condoms."

"Us?"

With a toss of her pink-banded head at the Ryder truck across the street, the Senior Campfire Girl said a brigade of "feministas" were gathering in the area "even as she spoke," and would be setting up camp near the OIC campus in the next day or so. "Too bad you'll miss the Rocky Mountain oyster fry, <u>Miss</u> So-and-So," she said, clearly meaning for the title "Miss" to be took as an insult. Watching her march out of the office, Henryetta reckoned G.G. Carpenter would be some surprised if she ever did get in direct contact with "Mr. Murphy," and him too. Sparks would sure enough fly between them. But it was doubtful that would ever happen, which was a shame, in a way. Though the *Femichismo!* editor was some younger, and her feminist point of view directly opposite of Mr. Shat's outlook on things, they might've made a semi-cute couple if they had met under less un-normal circumstances.

Henryetta, feeling better about her own self and cooled down some, went back to word processing Mr. Harold's "corker" of an editorial:

As of 1915, Marxist opposition to the Tsarist regime was split into two main factions: Bolsheviks, called "hards, led by Lenin, and Mensheviks, called "softs", led by a man named Martov. While the two groups shared the objective of doing away with the Romanovs, and private capital, Mensheviks favored relatively moderate means of transition to a new democratic order; the Bolsheviks espoused brutal violence and strict ideological dictatorship. The Bolshevik side prevailed, and in 1917 became the Communist Party.

From school days, some may recall "moderate" Marxism's last gasp as allegorically depicted by George Orwell's **Animal Farm,** *in which one leader of the revolution, a pig named "Snowball"—a/k/a Leon Trotsky, a Martov type—busily engaged in writing idealistic rules and planning a great windmill project, while another more radical revolutionary pig named "Napoleon"—a/k/a Lenin's successor, Joseph Stalin—raised cute little puppies, who grew into the ferocious hounds* *he ultimately unleashed upon his rival, Snowball.*

Let's hope, at the very least, that there are relatively moderate Mensheviks within the feminist revolutionary movement who will prevail over more radical militant elements. If not, one wonders if the Ballsheviks will be satisfied by anything less than ridding American college campuses of every red-blooded male they can lay their hands on.

Hmmm. Henryetta looked up, saw the big, boxy Ryder truck was gone, and went to wondering what G.G. Carpenter and her troop of "feministas" were up to.

TWENTY-FOUR

After standing at the window of her Dean's House office for yet another frustrating four-hour shift—in vain hope of seeing Martha Washington scamper back home from a prolonged tryst inside the OIC walls—Ester went to her desk, checked to see that a stapler there was fully loaded, and contemplated suicide. Her efforts to make real her feminist ideals by authority of Title IX had abjectly failed. Under her tutelage, only a single male on OIC's campus had shown modest signs of attitude and behavior correction in regard to proper relations with members of his opposite sex, which were now non-existent for all correctees, both male and female. That no rape epidemic had spread from other campuses was a statistical achievement of small consolation to Ester, given that she had been forced to impose strict segregation of genders following last week's disastrous launch of OIC's co-ed initiative. Women correctees were virtually cloistered like nuns in Cell Block F. Frat boys were similarly restrained elsewhere, which was gratifying to a degree, though their misogynistic old boys club "drinking" songs regularly wafted over the walls to torment her; as did the nauseating smell of bacon, despite her cease and desist orders to the kitchen staff. In utter despair, Ester let out a long sigh.

"I tol' you, Dean," said Demoana from her work station across the room: "The Governor wasn't gonna like you messin' with Coach Downs and the football team."

Yes, she was well aware of the disfavor with which she was now viewed from inside the State Capitol by both the Governor and—for more legitimate reasons—by her patron, the Lieutenant Governor. Equally distressing to Ester were the vicious personal attacks upon her made by unscrupulous radical elements of the feminist movement since her rise to Deanship seating status. Especially grating were the scurrilous onlline blogs, led by that bloody rag waved by a jealous former acquaintance at *Femichismo!*. If Greta Golightly Carpenter were to have been appointed Dean, OIC would now be modeled as not a prairie co-ed "Harvard of Correctology," but rather as a strictly same-sex prairie Wellesley. In G.G.'s radical hands, admittance of women to OIC would have been equivalent to the citizens of ancient Troy allowing a gift horse inside the city gates without looking into its orifices. G.G. Carpenter and her cohorts, all self described bitches, would have popped out and in short order male genitalia would have been eradicated from campus by whatever means necessary. They had once been friends, but...

"An' when that mean old senator puts in the paper he wants a woman put onto Death Row to satisfy his constitution, I get the feelin' he's talkin' about you, Dean Frigg."

Yes, that redneck jackass, Senator Lutz; what a hypocrite! What he really wanted was to have Coach Downs and the Wild Bunch football players set loose to take over OIC. He openly and proudly boasted that was once the case in the so-called glory days of Oklahoma University under a Coach Switzer. But one blunt prong of the dull-witted right-wing politician's vicious attack had hit a sore spot, Ester had to admit: Death Row at OIC was in fact an exclusive old boys club of sorts, in clear violation of women's Constitutional rights under Title IX. But what could she do about it? OIC's Death Row was her "Gitmo," in effect, only worse. Its members would eventually die of old age—she had even considered expediting the process—but new ones, all male, would inevitably qualify for admission to fill the ranks. The bastion of misogyny would carry on. She could just imagine the waft of an ongoing chorus: *My girl's from OIC/ She fights for her chastity/ Fights everyone but we/ The condemned men of Cell Block D.*

Again Ester sighed, then lifted the loaded stapler to her right temple. With Martha Washington gone missing and no one but Demoana Somebody for company, she was lonely. And so were the female co-eds bound to be, cooped in their quarters with only each other for companionship; as were, no doubt, the distressed male co-eds in their separate but equally distressed confinement. The collective frustrations of correctees—male and female—were nothing less than palpable. Unless something was done to reduce tension, who could say what might happen. Somehow, to save co-education at OIC, not to mention her career, a reconciliation of current gender disaffection needed to be brought about by some means. Ester herself had never felt such…such pent up yearning since her freshwoman year at Wellesley, finally relieved by…

"A mixer!" she exclaimed. The loaded stapler fell upon her desk. "Now that both male and female co-eds have had time to cool off…"

"Cool off?" said Demoana.

"…they should get a second chance in a less formal setting."

"They're like to be more het up."

"Not everyone will be invited," said Ester, on her feet, pacing. "Only those male co-eds who demonstrate model behavior between now and then will be admitted. Promise of pleasant mixing will motivate them. We shall have music and food."

"What about the gals?"

"To make certain the women are physically safe and secure, as well as protected from emotional or psychological trauma, male co-eds shall be sternly warned of being transferred to Death Row for any breach of my rules."

"I wouldn't be so worried about the women, as for the men, Dean Frigg. If you don't mind me sayin' so, I notice all your rules are against them."

Duh! Her hopelessly uneducated assistant could be so dense at times. Dealing with unacceptable <u>male</u> behavior was what Title IX was all about. Most of her rules, in essence, matched those adopted as law by the California state legislature for all public educational institutions. Yes, they created a broad legal presumption that virtually all physical contact, or suggestive words, made by men toward women constituted sexual assault. Yes, ambiguous courtship rituals dating back to the "jazz era" were kaput; there would be no more amor of the "she didn't say yes/ she didn't say no/ she didn't say stay/ she didn't say go" variety. However...

"Those gals will do just what they do since before you were born, Dean Frigg."

...lest anyone accuse Ester Frigg of being a party pooper, her rules allowed for plenty of amorous fun between genders by simply providing that women had to first give clear, fully informed-and-understood affirmative consent prior to each word and deed by a suitor, which consent was revokable at any time. Her rules did not go beyond bounds of common sense, such as those espoused by G.G. Carpenter. Under her stewardship, male correctees caught breathing heavily, whistling and staring at women who had not affirmatively consented to such initiatives would not <u>necessarily</u> be deemed rapists, as in the case of a radicalized Goshen College in Indiana. Such indicia of psychological rape—along with others, such as chewing pink gum, blowing bubbles, or uttering, under any circumstance, the word e-r-e-c-t-i-o-n—would simply be fairly judged by her personally—on a case-by-case basis—to be or not to be sexual assault.

"And I want to invite one or two of the male co-eds on Death Row to the mixer," said Ester, after returning to The Big, well-cushioned Chair. "They…"

"They are murderers, Dean Frigg," said Demoana. "Some of 'em must've killed women, and must have raped 'em too."

"I shall be highly selective," Ester replied, opening a file that lay on her desk. "Take this Mr. Jamus Murphy, for instance. He is a good deal older than the other male co-eds who will be in attendance, and comes to us by way of transfer from New Hampshire, my own home state. He is obviously a fun loving person of Black Irish descent, yet also has a certain Pennsylvania Dutch 'Amish' way about him. I myself have personally visited with Mr. Murphy, and know him to be a fine gentlemanly model for the young to emulate."

As had become her annoying nervous tic, Demoana rolled her eyes, implying a dubious attitude. But Ester knew what she was doing. Mr. Murphy had made a most favorable impression on her at their chance encounter during her search for Martha Washington. Indeed, she had later shoved a discreet fan card through the meal slot in his door, after he somehow managed to hold the door shut. Since then, occasionally passing by his cell, she had orally conveyed cordial greetings into his "bean hole." Mr. Murphy, like herself, was a New Englander, equally conservative in nature, politely reserved if not shy. Nevertheless, he had responded to her "open fan" signals with impassioned tapping in schoolboy code.

Blushing to imagine what TAP! TAP! TAP! obviously meant, Ester closed the file on Jamus Murphy and gave it a tender pat.

In answer to her request for guidance as to what special treat might be served at the mixer, Demoana said that in the town of McAlester a certain "King Fish" Somebody had a freezer full of of "prairie" oysters. How quaint; Ester was surprised such fare was available out there on the plain. When poor, uninformed Demoana further spoke — of an "oyster <u>fry</u>" — she could hardly keep herself from laughing. "For those who know no better, I suppose," Ester said, politely. "But as a New England girl, I much prefer mine raw. And to show the correctees their Dean is not a stick-in-the-mud sort, I may even shuck some myself. What fun!"

Needless to say, poor, dear Demoana rolled her eyes.

TWENTY-FIVE

Henryetta parked her Checker at a curb and hurried toward the *Weekly Herald*'s storefront office. She had drove down to OIC earlier in the afternoon to pick-up an installment of Mr. Shat's morality tale, **R***d Like Me**. The prison was on lock-down and no visitors were allowed in. But then Demoana said Buddy Brown—not confined to his cell because he was a trusty—was wanting to see her. She'd had a little heart flutter when Buddy came to the reception area, carrying a bow-tied gift box. But then he had again declined her suggestion that they go into the conjugatin' room to "chat" about this-and-that. "This is from Leon," he'd said, handing the box to her…Dang!…"and this is from me," he then said in a bashful way, likely blushing under his light brown skin, as he gave her an envelope. "Don't open it 'til you get to a private, safe and secure place," he whispered, with a wary glance from side to side. So she had hightailed back up the Indian Nation Turnpike. Now, seated at her semi-private, safe and secure *Weekly Herald* desk, she opened the envelope from Buddy:

SIMON PLASTER

Dean Frigg Cordially Invites You To A Co-Ed Mixer
Friday at 6:00 P.M. in the Rotunda
Refreshments, Music, Chains Optional

Dang! It was Friday afternoon already. Hmmm. Wondering what she should wear—all the other gals would be dressed in pink tops and bottoms—and whether the conjugatin' room would be available for any light sparkin' with Buddy, Henryetta opened the box from Leon. Inside, she found a stack of neatly folded sheets of toilet paper. At the top of the first page—its middle and bottom covered in Mr. Shat's handwriting—he had scrawled "URGENT!"

Henryetta began to read:

Yo! I say, Yo! I say, Yo! Yo!! Is anybody out there? It's me again, an oppressed African-American victim of sexual use and abuse on the Death Row of an institute of correctology that I dare not name. Is anybody outside these walls reading my morality tale, **R***d Like Me,** *written in my own precious body fluids on toilet paper and smuggled out of here by mule, at great risk to myself? I wonder. I wonder and I worry about my people, and about myself.*

Rabbit, one of the condemned bros riding with me on the Road to Yellow Mama, got a letter from his home bitch today. She told all about the hard partying still going on out there on the streets. Rabbit's ho, in the close company of Big Dick Bob, no doubt, is still "demonstrating" both in and outside the hood; shakin' her boot and grabbin' loot at keg parties themed "Black Lives Matter." She sent him a flyer put out by an organization on the march under that banner—Black Lives Matter—listing demands for action against cops who violate the rights and bodies of black people. Following are some of the zesty ones:

*"**We demand** a total independent investigative body that has full investigative powers…power to immediately sequester any and*

170

all police officers who are involved and/or are on the scene...full prosecuting power, and authority to mete out punishment.

__We demand__ that any and every officer accused of misconduct, abuse of authority, or the use of excess force be suspended immediately without pay, pending the outcome of independent investigation.

__We demand__ that any officer found guilty of any crime or violation while on duty be imprisoned and heavily fined personally, and any union that defends that officer be heavily fined with all money going to the victim.

__We demand__ body cams, vehicular cams, and cams on all weapons be live streamed to the public and controlled by an independent agency. All law enforcement agents must perform all duties and work in front of these cameras. Any officer found doing anything not in front of a camera shall be deemed guilty.

__We the people demand__ funding to establish independent community policing agencies.

__Let there be no surrender, no retreat, no compromising, no letting up and no excuses until all of our demands are met. Hold the line. Black Lives Matter!__"

Now of course, as an oppressed African-American man on Death Row, I am inclined toward the idea of frog-marching thousands of cops in front of kangaroo courts and putting them in prison. And I'm all for prying more coin from Fed coffers to spread around the hood. But what about me, an oppressed black man on Death Row? Sure as I'm sitting here in bacon stench, Rabbit's ho got stoned, scored a box of candy bars from a neighborhood convenience store before putting a torch to it, did some cool-down snarlin' with Big Dick Bob—a cracker slacker, I'd bet—and went on about her business 'til next hearty-party time on the street, without a thought to black lives inside these walls.

Wake up, my people! Wake up and smell the bacon! You can't make an effective poster boy out of an incident that not even the angry African-American Attorney General can find a way to call even a civil violation of civil rights. You can't make a believable morality tale without a reasonably bona fide victim, no matter how much media hype you get for the so-called demonstrations put on by professional protesters grinding other axes. If you want to get some justice done for oppressed African-Americans such as me, you've gotta yell "Rape! Rape! Rape!" like those feminista bitches are doing on college campuses. But no, the letter from Rabbit's double-deucing ho didn't contain a single word about we oppressed black men being unarmed to defend ourselves; no news of any hearty-party to protest brutal assaults on us by male gangbangers; and soon, very soon, by badass feministas wielding broomsticks, beer bottles and no doubt strap-on dildos. In the newspaper pictures included in the letter to Rabbit, not a single protester carried a sign saying **Black Anuses Matter Too!**

Meanwhile, on behalf of women, the Great Whore of Babylon — that pig, the Warden — has co-opted the essence of every single one of the African-American demands for justice, not for protection against cops, but for securing female feelings against assault by men's attentions. She, that short-legged, big-titted, round-eyed Persian witch, has already put in place a prison Office of Dispute Resolution ("ODR"), in which she alone is a self-appointed investigator, prosecutor, potential witness, judge and jury, with power to mete out punishment to male inmates for vaguely defined "sexual offenses" against women.

She has already issued two-hundred pages of rules, many of which she attempts to illustrate with references to heterosexual courtship as a friggin' "fan dance". Moves by male suitors, such as leerish looks in his eyes or suggestive double entendres hidden in what he says are either permissible or not, depending upon the manner in which the potential victim opens — not her mouth for a French lip lock --- but her "fan" intentions. How she spreads—not her legs for having a set of stones put to the gap—but her "fan" frame of mind. The Great Whore's rules are delicately designed to signal yes or no or maybe in terms of a potential female victim's mood from moment to moment, as sensed by her, not necessarily before or during zesty ingus, but also retroactively, perhaps years after the dirty deed was committed, never by her, always by a him. That's loony California law, but under a Fed statute called Title IX, Short Fat Fanny has got the doodads of us oppressed males in the same vice.

For crying out loud, according to one of the Country & Western Psalms in the Bible, there's always been women and whores and ladies; there's always been yeses and nos and maybes; from childhood, females start learning about teasing and squeezing and pleasing. Take it from somebody who has studied the Good Book and knows from experience: Hobble-de-gee and snarling has always been at least 99% under the control of the split-tails, who can put a guy out of the "mood" with a well timed fart; take down a giant Redwood with the flick of a finger. Are cameras mounted at the base of a man's hydraulic equipment really necessary? Our Warden has put in orders for such devices, and urges women to always assume positions during hobble-de-gee that will allow live streaming of their mood signals to the <u>public</u>.

On the other hand, I wouldn't complain if the new rituals of courtship required the feline Frigger to leave me alone. She passes by my cell almost hourly; says she's still searching for that darn cat. Came by only minutes ago; herself on the prowl for a randy "Tom" or "Dick." With no "fan" available for my protection, I coughed my head off, made retching sounds, shouted through the bean hole that I was infected with the Ebola virus. She peered in with a leerish look in a large round eye, and advised that a mouthful of those little blue, diamond-shaped pills would have me "up and about" in no time. In response, I had to also claim I was killing rattlesnakes that had slithered into my cell through an A/C duct, and would be busy later, skinning the reptiles for a pair of boots. She toodle-dooed through the bean hole and promised to return later for private "sensitivity training".

ARGHH! The horrid memory of it…I can't take it anymore! I want out! Pulitzer Prize be damned, I never should have put myself here in the first place. I'm not really black; that's just the color of my skin. My nappy hair, it's a wig; sewn to my scalp, but still, just a wig. Yes, I wrote the well received book, **Shat In A Black Man's Honda: Retracing The March From Selma By Car.** But that doesn't make me worthy to tell firsthand the story of an oppressed African-American man. I am not bona fide to be the poster boy for the black man's cause. Please believe me, I am wrongly incarcerated on Death Row of the Oklahoma Institute of Correctology, located on outskirts of the small town of McAlester. It's just off the Indian Nation Turnpike. Get me out of here, and _hurry_! The Great Whore of Babylon stalks me at this very moment.

Dear God, I know it wasn't You who made honky-tonk angels, but…

Henryetta looked up from Mr. Shat's manuscript, relieved to see Mr. Harold bob through the doorway. "Came back to get my fishin' license," he said. "It's weekend time, Henryetta; close up shop and come along with me out to Possum Pond."

She followed her boss to his desk, toilet paper in hand. "Mr. Harold, I'm dreadful worried about Mr. Shat, down there on that Death Row. His original way with words has got so off-colorful I can't rightly clean 'em up, and still hold firm to any sense of a morality tale. I fear he's having a mental breakdown or somethin.'"

"More likely havin' a little too much Who-Struck-John, if I know Shat. He's always been inclined to overdo, and…What are folks saying about my editorial?"

"Nothin', but listen to this," said Henryetta, paging through the toilet paper: "Mr. Shat wants someone to come down there right away and get him out. He sounds desperate and…Here, he says if he had wings of an angel, 'over these prison walls I'd fly,' then starts carryin' on about bein' a bird, sayin' good-bye to his own self: 'No one here can understand me. Oh the hard luck stories they all hand me…Pack up all my care and woe, here I go…Bye, bye, blackbird…' And then…"

"Well, I expect that's just Shat's original way with words again. You say folks aren't buzzin' about what I wrote from where I sit?"

"Mercy me! Mr. Harold! At the end of this here toilet paper, your old friend says if someone doesn't come to his rescue right away, he might as well…Mercy me, 'do the Dutch'!"

"Do the Dutch? Why, that's a dance step Shat introduced at college, from his hometown in the Pennsylvania Amish area west of Philadelphia. He must be clogging down there like a rock star."

"Nope, according to Mr. Shat, in a prison 'do the Dutch' is a cons' term for committing suicide!"

Mr. Harold went to rifling through a desk drawer and finally came up with the identification papers Mr. Shat had left with him: The "get-out-of-jail cards" that were to be handed to a warden after he'd finished writing **R***d Like Me**. "Uh oh," said her frazzled-looking boss. "According to today's *Tulsa World*, since that ruckus when those women were brought into OIC, the prison is still locked-down tighter than a mule's anus in fly season. No one from outside is allowed inside, for who can say how long."

Henryetta grabbed the get-out-of-jail-cards and Dean Frigg's mixer invitation; ran to her Checker, stomped on the gas pedal and took off lickety-split.

TWENTY-SIX

Coach Buster adjusted the stainless steel cup riding beneath his brand new, formal, pink-and-black spandex singlet—a game day uniform in official OIC colors—and looked around the Rotunda. For the "mixer" event that Dean Frigg had ordered him to attend, the lighting level had been lowered; pink-and-black streamers hung from the rails of the overhead walkways leading to and from cells; round paper lantern balls also dangled from above. Music began to drift in from somewhere, along with a few male inmates; none of them in chains. Feeling more uneasy, Coach again adjusted his family jewels protector. The scene reminded him of the one for a high school "prom" event he had spied on through a window following his graduation. As female inmates, also unchained, arrived in droves, he feared that at this "mixer" event also, dancing might break-out at any moment. And that made him more and more nervous.

He had been raised Southern Baptist by his mother; made to go to church every week and sit through terrifying warnings about hell and damnation. Now his shoulders twitched, he adjusted his cup, at recollection of staying home sick one Sunday.

His mother got back from church and re-told a sermon the preacher had bellowed from the pulpit about an experience he'd recently had. According to the preacher man, said his mother, he and his wife had returned home from a night at the movies, turned on living room lights, and found their teenaged daughter and her boyfriend "rasslin'" on a couch, with no clothes on. Ordered to explain themselves, they admitted they had been "making love." The preacher said he was relieved. "Thank God," he yelled, "for a minute I thought they might have been <u>dancing</u>!" So Coach Buster had never set foot on a dance floor, not even after his mother told him twenty years later that she had told the "old joke" about the sermon 'cause she didn't want him to get distracted from his rasslin' by any nonsense such as dancing. Again, he adjusted his cup and looked around.

Off to one side of the big round room, smoke billowed up from a deep-fry cooker. A new odor filled the space. He was glad to see that it was Rocky Moutain oysters being fried. Bacon smell had got to be a big pollution problem at OIC. Earlier that day, two football players had vomited onto the practice field after a cloud of grease dripped down on the squad. Like about everyone else, he hoped the environmental engineers would soon get finished with using pigs to test the new electric chair, and that so-called "Mama Megawatt" would have enough wind-powered voltage to get put into operation for its intended purpose. None of the Wild Bunch players were on Death Row, and with the opening game against the Colorado Cutthroats coming up..."Isn't it grand to see our male and female co-eds mixing so well," said Dean Frigg, who had sidled up beside him; out of her regular pinstriped pantsuit and into a bright red dress; her hair out of its usual ball on top of her head and hanging down on her shoulders.

Coach noticed that in fact more male and female inmates had bunched up into mixed groups. Music got louder and everyone started to…"Shall we join the fun?" said the Dean, with a big smile of her bright red lips that matched the color of her dress, and high-heeled shoes. Before he could think of a way to just say no, she got an arm around to his back, grabbed a hand, and started into what felt like a Reverse T&A Trap move. It was all he could do to resist his trained instinct to counter with a Stand & Deliver head-butt to her chest. "I think it's important that we faculty members set a good example," she said, switching to what would have been an effective Side Rider if she'd had the arm strength of Georgette.

"Push it! Push it! Push it!" a circle of exercising inmates around them chanted, as he shifted his weight from foot to foot in a Standing Ball Change step. "Push it! Push it! Push it!" Thankfully, his jockstrap and cup held firm inside the new singlet. "Push it! Push it! Push it!"

"I bear glad tidings, Coach Downs," said the Dean. "That white, uh, 'Studback' of yours has shown great progress in my Sensitivity Class, and as a budding Muslim jihadi will now meet my diversity requirement. I look forward to seeing him — how do you say it? — 'throw a long bomb' in the upcoming game."

"<u>White</u> studback?"

"Why yes, Mr. Corn of course. See to it that he is suitably rewarded for his academic achievement. OIC now is, after all, well on its way to becoming truly the prairie 'Harvard of Correctology'."

"Push it! Push it! Push it real good, baby, baby."

As the Dean scanned the smoky room, as though in search of a different work-out partner, she loosened her grip. Buster did the same, looking for Georgette. As the music got louder and smoke from the deep-fry cooker got thicker, they drifted apart.

"Who dat? Who dat?"

"Rock wit it! Rock wit it!"

"Do dat. Do dat."

"Push it! Push it! Push it!"

"Push it real good, baby, baaaby."

"Crank this. Crank that."

"Shake your booty, baaaaby!"

Georgette appeared out of the smoke, just like his mother used to make her entrance out of a steamy shute from locker room toward the wrestling ring. In an all-pink, low-neck singlet, with matching ribbons tied to her braided blonde pigtails, she looked as good or better than Daisy Mae Bernstein—The Human Pig Sticker—who he had pinned in her maiden match with a nifty Deep Stick move of his own.

"Who dat? Who dat?"

"Rock wit it! Rock wit it!"

Georgette Crabwalked up to him. "Wanna bust a move or two, Coach?"

Bust a move? The time and place didn't seem right for mixing it up on the "mat," much as he would have liked to. On the other hand, it looked like all the inmates, and even Dean Frigg across the now crowded, smoky room, were loosening up for a full-bore winner-take-all rassle-rama-rama event.

What the heck, he struck a Crouching Dragon pose and moved left.

"Do dis. Do dat."

Georgette went into a Standing Tiger position.

"Rock wit it! Rock wit it!"

He did a backward Swag Walk.

Georgette spun into a Whirling Dervish maneuver.

"Push it! Push it! Push it!"

He moved in on her with a left-footed Leg Glider feint.

She took him down with a Running Lunger.

"Get your freak on, baaaby!"

"Crank it, crank it, baaaby!"

"Rock wit it! Rock wit it!"

Coach Buster, rolling around on the floor with Georgette in a double Asian Wraparound hold—both of them sweating and groaning—couldn't remember when he'd had such an even fair-and-square free-style match without an uptight referee buttin' in.

TWENTY-SEVEN

Months of driving on slick tires finally caught up to Henryetta, so at a slowed-down speed she had poked along for the last ten miles to OIC on the rims of the right-side wheels of her Checker. Fearing she would be too late to get into Dean Frigg's mixer, and get Mr. Shat out of the locked-down institute, she ran from the visitor parking lot toward the prison walls. At the check-in desk, a guard let her in—thanks to the printed invitation Buddy Brown had slipped to her on the sly—and from loud racket coming through a corridor from the Rotunda, she could tell there was a party going on. Running down the long hallway filled with smoke, she about gagged on the odor of, not bacon this time; the semi-sweet aroma smelled more like that of Rocky Mountain oysters gettin' fried.

Sure enough, in the also smoky Rotunda, she found Demoana overseeing a deep-fry cooker, staffed by…"Land sakes alive, Leon, is that you?" she said to a different-looking Leon. "What's happened to you?" In the two weeks since she'd seen him in the conjugatin' room, he had thinned down and cut-off his ratty red beard. Now his face matched his also shaved head;

and there was somethin' else different about him. When he smiled back at her and moved his lips—in all the noise around her, Henryetta couldn't hear what he said—but to her own shock, she thought Leon Corn had got to be downright semi-handsome. If the boiling cooker hadn't been between them, she might have gave him a big hug, or— stranger than lipstick on a pig—she might've even asked him to dance.

"Whew!" said Demoana, fanning herself with a hand and moving away from the hot spot. Henryetta did the same, and asked if Dean Frigg was at the crowded party. "Oh yeah, she's here somewhere, dressed up like a cardinal bird and twerkin' on the dance floor last time I seen her." In answer to Henryetta admitting that she wasn't up to date on the dance steps that went with what must have been hip-hop music blasting out of a big boom box, Demoana pointed out a young gal in the crowd as a demonstrator of "twerking;" to another female inmate as "jerking;" to another as doing the "Heavy D Shake." From Henryetta's point of view, most of the moves she saw looked like plain ol' whooppee. "That gal over there with her shirt off is doin' the Swag Surf up against that boy's Electric Slide," Demoana explained. "And that couple down on the floor in tight underwear, hers pink and his OIC colors—you can barely see 'em 'through all the naked legs dancin' around 'em—they doin' the Humpy, which is about the same thing as…"

Land sakes alive! Mr. Shat, holding two large plastic cups in his hands, was there; semi-shuckin'-and-jivin' with a youngish gal. Relieved that he was still alive, Henryetta headed in his direction and…Land sakes alive again! G.G. Carpenter had somehow got into the mixer, must have identified Mr. Shat as Jamus Murphy—her link to "Sheep Dog"—and was movin' toward him like a she-wolf in white pantsuit and pink headband, stalking an innocent black lamb. They got to him at the same time, but Ms. Carpenter got "Mr. Murphy's" attention first.

"Shat, is that you?" the *Feminismo!* editor said, staring at him with her bright blue eyes. "My Goddess, you look…somehow different. What's happened to you? And what are you doing here at this…this…Is this some kind of military academy?"

Seeming none surprised to see her, Mr. Shat smiled. "Gigi," he said, "you've changed your hair."

"I cut it off for you, Shat. After you dumped me—followed by two more years of sexual abuse by all the other male bosses at *Newsweek*—I gave up on men. Now I am…"

"Gigi, you don't mean to say a yeasty slice like you turned…"

"I'm not homo, but I'm not hetero anymore either. I'm just neutero, and bitter. It's all your fault, Shat; you broke my heart."

"You had it coming, Gigi. You were my protege, I showed you the ropes. All the thanks I got—in addition to twice-a-day hobble-de-gee—was a knife in the back; not once, not twice, but…"

"Shat, I was too young to understand the tricks of journalism back then. Now I know…"

"You stabbed me in the back, Gigi; not once, not…"

"Shat, for cryin' out loud, I was the *Newsweek* <u>fact</u> checker; I was doing my job! And really, Shat—'Four score and forty years ago'?—the math of was all wrong for age of a dying mother with a young child, but I let your first-person account slide."

"Okay, you stabbed me in the back only nine times."

"C'mon, Shat, gimme a break. Your 'eye-witness' Katrina story was great, but, uh, some of the colorful little details… No African-American orphans got their throats slashed inside the New Orleans Superdome; George W. Bush didn't rape their mothers on the fifty-yard line; and to say Robert E. Lee was responsible for the FEMA fuck-up was quite a stretch even for you."

"I wrote partly what the *Times-Picayune* reported, and partly what I got from another eye-witness source—savvy TV guy with a long nose for news—hangin' around a reliable bar on Bourbon Street."

Mr. Shat gulped down whatever was in one plastic cup; then emptied the other down his gullet. "No hard feelings, Gigi," he then said. "You did what you thought was right, for your career, not mine."

"No, Shat, I was wrong, terribly wrong. I see that now."

"You look good, Gigi. I've missed you."

"They're playing our song, Shat. Shall we dance?"

As Mr. Shat and "Gigi" Carpenter got to jerking or twerking or whatever, Henryetta spotted Dean Frigg across the room; a red dress strapped onto her body and hair down around her shoulders. With Mr. Shat's "get out of jail" papers in the hip pocket of her jeans, she set out to…Uh oh, Dean Frigg came flying at Mr. Shat and Ms. Carpenter like an angry red bird; lit down between them, and started screeching. Henryetta moved closer to hear what was said.

"I said get out!" said the Dean. "This is a by-invitation-only private party, Gigi, and I have already promised this dance to Mr. Murphy."

"Oh, for cryin' out loud, Ester," said Ms. Carpenter. "His name's not 'Murphy' and I got him first."

"You once claimed first dibs meant nothing in love and war, as I recall. I was taking care of the injured Yale lacrosse player. You butted in, grabbed the handles to his wheel chair and…"

"Gimme a break, Ester. That was thirty years ago at that dumb Wellesley mixer you set up. The Yalie wanted to dance, and let's face it: You were never much of a rock-n-roller."

"I saw him first," Dean Frigg insisted, with a glance at Mr. Shat. "Now it's my turn to dance, you back-stabbing bitch!"

"No, I saw this one first," said Ms. Carpenter, also with a glance. "I was banging Shat twice a day when you were no doubt a still sexually frustrated thirty-year-old virgin struggling through graduate school. And besides, you had your turn. You pulled that Yalie out of the wheel chair and dragged him into the bushes. From a balcony, we all watched you try to have your way with him. What a ghastly sight that was!"

"I thought he was a slightly injured lacrosse player! I didn't know he was paralyzed from the neck down. And anyway," Dean Frigg said, cozying up to Mr. Shat, who had somehow got hold of two more large cups of beverage, "I am in charge here, Gigi. Mr. Murphy knows me as 'Ester' and I affectionately refer to him as my 'Sheet Dog'."

With a startled look in her pretty blue eyes, Ms. Carpenter gazed at Mr. Shat for a second, then stared at Dean Frigg with fire in her eyes. "'Sheep Dog' is _my_ exclusive source!" she shouted, before lunging to grab hold of the Dean's hair with both hands. Mr. Shat turned and hotfooted through a pocket of denser smoke, probably headed back to his cell on Death Row. G.G. Carpenter took off after him. Dean Frigg got back on her feet. "Dean, I hate to bother you during a social occasion," said Henryetta, taking Mr. Shat's true identity papers out of her pocket, "but if you would just have a look at these here get-out-of-jail documents..."

As OIC's top dog also headed into the smoke, Henryetta reckoned she might as well find Buddy Brown and have some fun while she waited for the two ex-college-roommates to sort things out.

About fifteen minutes later she had Buddy pinned against

a wall of the corridor leading to the conjugatin' room. "Thank you, Miss Henryetta," he said, after she released him from an open-mouth lip-lock. "May I kiss you back, Miss Henryetta?" Though the trusty inmate's overly polite manners were becoming semi-tiresome to her, she nudged him farther down the hallway, kicked the conjugatin' room door open, and pushed him into the darkened love nest. A light came on. "Arghhh!" Buddy cried, before turning back, pushing her to the side, and hightailing it back toward the Rotunda.

Henryetta stuck her head through the doorway. Land sakes alive! Standing on the bed in her red high-heeled shoes, Dean Frigg lifted the skirt of her dress, like she was fixing to set down on Mr. Shat's face or somethin'! G.G. Carpenter held his legs down—after she'd already pulled off his pants, by the look of things—and was gettin' busy in his privates area, with what might have been a nail file in her hand!

Appreciating how such a sight might have knocked Buddy Brown out of the mood for sparkin'—maybe for the rest of his life—Henryetta her own self took off for the Rotunda to find an armed guard to help poor Mr. Shat out of the fix he was in.

TWENTY-EIGHT

The single dim bulb in Shat's cell had blinked off-and-on well past midnight. Odor of bacon was intense. All was deathly quiet on Death Row, as he continued to pace the floor like a caged animal awaiting slaughter at dawn. Still shaken by the attempted assault on his hydraulics, and face — thanks to oyster-fry smoke, a fire alarm bell had saved him from completed rape — he continued to assess his predicament: He was not a poor little lamb who had lost its way; oh no, he was a certain somebody's "Sheep Dog"! Outside the walls, he wouldn't mind hooking up with Gigi again — she was still yeasty! — but if forced to remain inside OIC he would damn sure mind becoming Ester Frigg's twice-a-day hobble-de-gee bitch! If only he had available to him the rigged system she had set up for female rape victims, without all that Constitutional bullshit about due process of law, he would have his revenge. Alas, that was not an option in his case. The Great Whore's rules didn't recognize the possibility that males could be sex assault victims. But once he got outside the walls, where fair law and order ruled, he would report Frigg — not Gigi — to police. He would see her put in a courtroom dock and...

Or maybe not. Even in the free world, people might not find his victimhood story credible. Even worse, Shat now realized, would be his humiliation if they <u>did</u> believe his true story! Hell, some unscrupulous news reporter might even put his name in a newspaper, maybe a picture. For cryin' out loud, he'd planned to attend a college class reunion back at "Old Nassau" in September. What would the fellas at Tiger Inn think of a guy who had suffered only attempted rape at the hands of a woman, or two? Zesty completion of the crime would sound better, but what would be the equivalent opposite of "penetration"? Yes, now that he thought more about his traumatic experience, Shat realized that he had indeed been led into a full blown act of ingus, for which he had not been in the mood. He had indeed been raped. That was his story, and he would stick to it.

The girl, Henryetta, had been at last night's mixer. From the desperate look on her slightly freckled face, he could tell she'd read his recent cry for freedom. No doubt by noon he would be saved from OIC and the sharp-clawed, furry clutches of Dean Frigg. Hallelujah! Back on the street, he would...Recollection that he was out of a job, and broke, stopped Shat in his tracks. His latest journalistic effort, **R***d Like Me**, as written, was bound to be a loser, he realized. Nobody cared anymore about the oppressed black man. That age-old morality tale had gotten stale. The current President was African-American, for cryin' out loud; so were the most adored American heros of recent decades: Bill Cosby, Colin Powell, Michael Jordan, O.J. Simpson and The Grand Old Oprah of course. The list was endless. And a mug shot of the Reverend Jimbo Sharpster on a promo of the oppressed black man tale wouldn't have quite the appeal of a Martin Luther King, Junior's face back in the day of Selma.

In despair, Shat flopped onto his concrete cot...

Minutes after the blow to his head, he regained consciousness and went back to dwelling on his plight. He had hitched his wagon onto the stooped shoulders of the so-called oppressed African-American man and now the joy ride was over. The feminist narrative of women's resistance to oppression by an unjust patriarchal system had sped by him like a "Lesburu Outback" plastered with compelling slogans—WOMEN DESERVE OBAMACARE DILDOS and BEND OVER/HERE IT COMES!—but he'd been asleep at the reins in the slow lane of journalism. Currently, the feminista morality tale of a rampant rape epidemic on college campuses had captured...

Shat's aching head popped up from the concrete pillow. Hell, he himself had been on "campus" for three long weeks. He himself had been truly raped. With the recent admission of women to OIC, the co-ed sex assault epidemic was bound to spread to where he lay. The story could be bigger than the one about Duke lacrosse players that *The New York Times* flogged for weeks, or the more recent *Rolling Stone* semi-first-person exposé of a brutal frat house rape at the University of Virginia. And he already had the makings in hand for a truly first-person bombshell. For a head shot on such a book's back cover, he could don a long blonde wig, maybe horn-rimmed grasses. He could adopt a *nom d' plume*, say, the married name of his disappeared twin sister.

Shat got up from the prison Cadillac, excited by his new idea for changing his tune and pepping up his career. With a few legitimate journalistic liberties—mainly artful re-working of small gender details in an honest account of last night's true life experience—he could edit **R***d Like Me**. He could get on the feminista bandwagon, perhaps in the back seat, so to speak, with Gigi. Yes, though he'd been late to grasp Jamus "Sheep Dog"

Murphy's wise advice—he had not immediately known when to hold and when to fold the cards dealt to him—he still knew how to pull an ace out of a body cavity. Ignoring the renewed off-and-on blinks of the light in his cell, Shat sat on the lidless crapper, unspooled a yard of toilet paper, and began to write:

R***D LIKE ME
by
Ms. Shitner Poole

Baa, baa, baa. I'm a poor little lamb who got rolled in the hay. Baa, baa, baa. I'm a little lost sheep who cried nay means nay. Baa, baa, baa…

TWENTY-NINE

In the back seat of her Checker, still parked in the OIC visitors lot, Henryetta woke up at dawn to the sound of singing and the smell of burning rubber. She sat up, rubbed sleep from her eyes, and saw black smoke rising from inside the correctology institute. *We go to college, to college go we/ We go to college…*Land sakes alive! Dozens of soldiers in army camouflage outfits were on top of the walls, and others were climbing up ropes, singing what sounded like another one of those old frat songs. *We go to college, oil up your gun/ We'll show you boys, how it oughta be done/ We watched the movies, in sex ed A-one/ We're the women of OIC!* Henryetta made sure she had Mr. Shat's get-out-of-jail papers still in her hip pocket, then ran toward the commotion.

We go to college, we are oversexed/ Just get in line boys, you may be next/ We are highly rated, we are educated/ We are the women of OIC!

Up closer, Henryetta could see that although all the soldiers had short hair, they were gals alright. And all of 'em wore pink headbands like G.G. Carpenter's. Three days ago, the *Feminismo!* editor had said a bunch of feministas were gathering in the area, so this must be them, Henryetta reckoned, as she got to the OIC visitors entrance.

And once a week at the college dance/ We don't wear bras and we don't wear pants/ We always give the boys a fighting chance/ We are the women of OIC!

Inside, there were no guards at the check-in desk. Henryetta turned around and saw more of Ms. Carpenter's gals coming in behind her, all singing.

The OIC boys, they are a bunch of sissies/ They get worked up, from one or two kisses/ It takes wax candles, and broomstick handles/ To rouse the women of OIC!

She ran from them, down the corridor toward the Rotunda. In there, a smoky bonfire burned. A big boxy Ryder truck was backed up to it, and from the open rear of the truck, gals were emptying boxes of…They were burning hundreds of those foam rubber brassiere inserts called "falsies" that her mother, Wynona Sue, was inclined to wear on first dates. Across the big round room…Uh oh. Nine or ten OIC guards were lined up, lookin' like possums caught in headlights. A group of feministas were down on their knees, putting manacles on the guards' ankles. Trying to keep their prisoners calm or somethin', they sang a softer-sounding sorta serenade:

Do your balls hang low? Do they swing to and fro?/ Can you tie 'em in a knot? Can you tie 'em in a bow?

Can you throw 'em o'er your shoulder/ like a macho-man soldier?/ Can you do the double shuffle when your balls hang low?

Then, sure enough, G.G. Carpenter, still dressed in the white pantsuit from the night before—now smudged with soot—started climbing up to a platform that had been put on sawhorses. The hobbled guards shuffled past her.

Would they make a lusty clamor if we hit 'em with a hammer?/

Would they make a hollow sound if you dragged 'em on the ground?

Would you feel a mellow tingle if we hit 'em with a shingle?/ Would they make you stand tall if we bounced 'em off a wall?

Would they sound like a gong if we pulled upon your dong?/ Can you do the double shuffle when your balls hang low?

"HOOAH!" G.G. Carpenter shouted through one of two microphones standing on the platform with her.

Hooah! yelled at least sixty or seventy "Senior Campfire Girls," circled below her. Henryetta now reckoned for sure they were a band of radical feminist Ballsheviks that Mr. Harold had warned about.

"WHAT DO WE WANT?"

Justice!

"WHEN DO WE WANT IT?

Bohica! Bohica! Bohica!

"HOW DO WE GET IT?"

Off with their heads!

Off with their heads!

Off with their heads!

We are the dirty bitches of OIC/ And you can tell by the smell that we're not feeling well/ When the end of the month rolls around.

For it's hi, hi, hee in the tampon industry/ Shout out your sizes loud and strong.

Regular!

Super-Duper!

Bail of Hay!

For where 'ere we go, we will let men know/ When the end of the month rolls around!

G.G. Carpenter climbed down from the platform. Henryetta hustled over to her. "What in tarnation is goin' on?" she asked. "I hate to say it, Ms. Carpenter, but you are bound to be breakin' laws hand over fist!"

"They're not our laws," the radical feminista answered, cool as a breeze blowed in from the Rocky Mountains. "It's a revolution, H.E. You had your chance to be part of it, but got your panties twisted about a few petty propaganda details. I was once young and dumb like you, but...Last night, seeing Shat again after all these years, I admit: Even I wavered for a minute or two, until Ester Frigg tipped her hand. Obviously—though incredibly—she's trapped 'Mr. Murphy' in her honey pot. She knows or suspects he's onto 'Sheep Dog's' story and has either already coaxed him to reveal the victim's identity, or is trying to. No matter. We don't need him anymore, now that we're in control of OIC. We will find 'Sheep Dog' on our own; publish her story to create more panic on other college campuses. And further disgrace, Ester Frigg, of course."

"Where is Dean Frigg?"

"In retreat, I imagine. I am now in charge. Justice shall be done *en masse* within the hour."

We are the dirty bitches of OIC/ You can tell by our eyes that there's blood between our thighs/ You can tell by our stance we've got a rag in our pants/ When the end of the month rolls around.

For it's hi, hi, hee in the tampon industry/ Shout out your sizes loud and strong...

G.G. Carpenter looked over her shoulder for a second. "Ester is wily as a Persian; sure to mount a counter-attack," she then said. "As I tried to make you understand, H.E., there is a civil war going on between our side and wishy-washy 'Shiite' feminists such as Ester Frigg. Cut your hair, grab a headband and join us! There's still time for you to stand up and be counted as loyal to the true cause of your gender, but it's running out fast."

Henryetta reckoned there would be no point to her gettin'

Mr. Shat's identification papers out of her pocket. "Gigi" already knew he wasn't no Jamus Murphy from New Hampshire, and she clearly wasn't inclined to be kindly toward him. But Dean Frigg seemed to be sweet on Mr. Shat; more likely to let him out of jail if she got back control of OIC; and she was bound to make a counter-attack. So although Henryetta knew journalists were not supposed to take sides, she was hopeful the Dean's "Shiite" wing of feminism would win the civil war.

THIRTY

Ester, still dressed in the red party frock and high-heeled shoes she'd worn to last night's mixer, lay sprawled face-down on her bed. An eyelid came unstuck from a gob of dark mascara. Initially, she was relieved—Martha Washington writhing in the clutches of Mama Megawatt had been only a terrible nightmare—but now she distinctly detected what she thought was an odor of burning hair. She struggled to her feet and staggered to a window. At the horrifying sight of black smoke across the way, she shrank from the window and fell backward onto the bed, face up. "Demoana!" she shrieked. Immediately, her slow-footed assistant came into the bedroom, with bad news written all over her round black face. So it was true: Martha Washington had been lured into Death Row and...

"I been tryin' to wake you, Dean Frigg, but there was an awful lot of Friendly Creature in that punch you made up for last night's big mixin' party. Ten guards, draggin' chains, are waitin' downstairs for you to tell 'em what to do. The pris...The campus has been took over by that long-legged, short-haired woman in the white pantsuit and her soldiers."

What?! Ester got to her feet and returned to the window. So it was true; the bad news was written in black smoke across a clear blue sky: Greta Golightly Carpenter and her radical feminist followers had seized control of OIC. But for the sticky mascara clogging her tear ducts, Ester would have wept in pity for herself. Gigi-the-Carpenter, her longtime rival, had thwarted her noble effort to prove that sensible application of so called "moderate" feminist ideology could create a civilized new structure for gender relations on college campuses. More importantly, the conniving short-haired bitch had made her look weak and ineffective. Her reputation, her tenure as OIC Dean, her career; all were going up in noxious smoke. With Martha Washington gone missing, she would have nothing to live for. "Demoana!" she shrieked at her assistant, standing immediately behind her. "Get your blackboard and follow me into the breach!"

The manacled guards, clanking as they shuffled, carried Ester—seated firmly in The Big Chair—inside the walls through a gate and into the Rotunda by way of a back doorway, both of which had been left open. As she moved through the smoky haze filling the large interior space, both female correctees in pink uniforms and G.G.'s feministas in camouflage outfits made way for her passage. Lights flickered off and on. A bonfire petered out. From somewhere, a dog howled. The bitch, G.G, in a dirty white pantsuit, stood atop a makeshift platform; arms folded, looking down at..."That be Freemo, main man of the A.D. gang," Demoana said. At a standing microphone set on the Rotunda floor, a highly animated female co-ed, donned in a headrag, ranted at the surly-looking thug, "Mister Freemo":

"You be climbin' in our windows. You be snatchin' our peoples up. Tryin' to rape everybody in here. So we all need to hide our self, hide our sister. Hide our self, hide our sister. Hide our self, hide our sister. 'Cause you been rapin' eveybody 'round here. You don't have to confess. We heard you, we heard you, homeboy. You so dumb, you so dumb…"

"Silence!" Ester bellowed. Quiet fell over the large assembly, as the guards hoisted her, in The Big Chair, onto the platform. "Oh for cryin' out loud," said Gigi. "Ester, you look ridiculous in that get-up from last night: Like Jabba the Harlot Hut; utterly grotesque. Go home and take a shower. There's a rape trial in progress, the first of many."

Rape trial? Had the campus rape epidemic spread to OIC? "If you had been on the ball last night," said Gigi, "doing your job instead of boozing and making a spectacle of yourself on the dance floor, you might have noticed—right under your powdered nose—commission of multiple sex assaults of every gross nature under the sun. This man in the dock, for instance, Mr. Freemo, leader of…"

Down with penises! Down with penises! Down with penises! Down with…

"Silence in the court!" Ester shouted into a second handy microphone set on the platform. "I am in total charge of these proceedings."

She turned to the short-haired would-be usurper of her authority, G.G. Carpenter. "You are a fool, Gigi," she said, "and your radical revolution is badly misguided. There was no need for violent civil and criminal disobedience by you and your band of bandits. Title IX has already broken all the laws necessary, and then some! The feminist war against men has been virtually won by stealthy strategy. And I am the official Title IX enforcement officer, head of the OIC ODR, fully authorized by the Feds to act as investigator, prosecutor, judge, jury and executioner in all matters of gender dispute, including accusations of sexual assault of every gross nature under both sun and moon. I am also just as strong a feminist as you, Gigi. I can be just as bloody a jihadi as you."

"Prove it!" Gigi shouted. "I don't think you've got the stones to off the heads of these misogynist pricks."

Down with pricks! Down with pricks! Down with pricks! Down with...

"The court is now in proper order!" Ester proclaimed. "The witness may continue with her accusations against the sex assaulter, Mr. Freemo."

"He be climbin' in our windows. He be snatchin' our peoples up. Hide your self, hide your sister. Hide your self, hide your sister. Hide yourself, hide your sister. 'Cause he been rapin' everybody 'round here. He so dumb. Run an' tell that, homeboy. You so dumb, you so dumb, you don't have to confess 'cause..."

"Enough!" Somewhat hazily, Ester recalled the young victim as having been one of the more expressive dancers at last night's mixer, but did not recall seeing..."We wasn't even here wit dese skanky hos," said the presumably guilty defendant. "Me and my homeboys was on lock-down, uninvited to be witch the bitches."

Down with snatchers! Down with snatchers! Down with...

As though caught in the act of minor embellishment of fact, the witness looked up with big round eyes, then turned toward Gigi for a second before continuing: "When the electricity went out and the boom box died, I heard the homeboys out there singin' that hurtful song 'bout rolling me over an' doin' it again, an' doin' it again. Rollin' me over an' doin' it again, an' doin' it again, which triggered a painful trombone in me."

Down with boners! Down with boners! Down with boners! Down with...

"Yes, triggering 'trauma' is sexual assault alright," Ester

declared. "Write that down, Demoana."

"T-h-a-t," her assistant mumbled, as she chalked her slate.

Down with triggers! Down with triggers! Down with triggers! Down with...

"But what are you going to do about it, Ester," said Gigi; "cut the frat boy some slack 'cause his daddy, 'Mr. Big Balls', is no doubt an alum of OIC?"

Down with Misters! Down with Misters! Down with Misters! Down with...

Ester glared at the obviously guilty defendant and twenty or twenty-five bros gathered 'round him, all wearing pink-and-black-banded straw boater hats; all striking defiant slouching poses, all sneering at her. "I hereby find the entire A.D. fraternity guilty in the first degree!" she declared. "Mr. Freemo and all members of his club shall be expelled from OIC forthwith. Guards step forward. Off with their heads!"

"Hey, judgette, you are violating my rights of due process," the rapist cried, sounding less of the hood association as of the bar association. "I was not given benefit of legal counsel; I was not allowed to cross-examine the accuser or testify in my own behalf. So what if the ho heard us singing; that's hearsay. The A.D. Club is private, unconnected to OIC and not subject to Title IX. My father is an OIC alum, and a lawyer, who will sue your honky ass for kicking us out of his *alma mater.* I protest!"

"Don't write that down," Ester said to Demoana, before glancing at Gigi and bellowing: "Next case!"

"Off with their heads! Next case."

"Off with their heads! Next case."

"Off with their heads! Next case."

"Off with their heads! Next case."

"Off with their heads! Next case."

"Off with their heads! Next case."

"Off with their heads!"

Based firmly on the expert opinion of numerous feminist authorities—that the type of adolescent males who joined frats were prone to getting shit-faced drunk, and certain to commit sexual assaults—in a matter of thirty minutes or so, Ester had additionally ridded the OIC campus of Bloods, Crips, Aryan Brothers, Netas, Black Guerillas, Jewish Jihadis, Badass Bohicas and Phi Lamda Philatelists. Not yet sure, however, that she had quenched her rival feminist's thirst for male blood, she next shouted: "Bring on the jocks!"

Down with jocks! Down with cocks! Down with jocks! Down with cocks! Down...

Minutes later: "Off with their heads!"

Ester sighed with satisfaction. What fun to have dispatched the entire brutish team comprised of "H-backs" and "Studbacks" and "tackles" and" linebackers" and other football players to low wage careers in the outside world more suited to their lack of intelligence and worthwhile talents. Too bad OIC had no preppy lacrosse players on campus.

"Nice wet work, Ester," said Gigi, still on the platform beside her. "But impersonal mass executions are pieces of cake. Have you got the stone cold cojones to look individual rapists in the eye and bring down the hammer, or do I need to take it from here?"

Down with hammers! Down with nails! Down with...

"Bring on the individual heads!" Ester shouted, whereupon a line of perhaps a hundred male co-eds was immediately formed in front of the platform. Looking into the eyes of each—none of whom she recognized as a person worthy of much attention—she sent them packing one by one with little fanfare. Near the tail end of the queue, however, came three rapists in whom she had a personal interest.

"Ah, Mr. Rabbit from Death Row, I see. Was it not you who whistled through your bean hole as I passed by your cell?"

"I was only admiring your fine ass, Dean Frigg. Please don't…"

"You are out of here, Rabbit! Next case."

"I know what you're gonna say," said Mr. Greasy, also from Death Row. "But that was a frankfurter I stuck out of my bean hole, for your cat. You looked a lot like your cat from that angle."

Down with weiners! Down with weiners! Down with weiners! Down with…

"Off with the head of this weiner!" Ester ordered, before looking into the evil eyes of Mr. Raw Dawg.

"Speaking of Martha Washington," she said to the third Death Row correctee, "a little bird told me you were heard to call 'pussy, pussy, pussy' to her as she pranced by your cell next door to Mama Megawatt, and that was shortly before her disappearance. Heretofore, you have not denied the charge, and have claimed so-called Fifth Amendment protection against self incrimination. Has the waterboarding therapy brought you to your senses?"

"Okay, okay," he said, red-faced with shame. Ester braced herself for the awful truth about Martha Washington's cruel fate. "I admit I called out to her through my bean hole," said the disgusting pervert, "but I thought it was <u>you</u> walking by, not that darn cat. And…and all I wanted was to smell your hair. I never touched, or even sniffed your cute little p…"

Down with noses! Down with sniffers! Down with dorks! Down with…

"Sentence now, verdict later!" Ester bellowed. "Guards!

Shuffle this bad boy home to Mama Megawatt on Death Row!"

"My Goddess, Ester!" said G.G. Carpenter, leaning on the shaft of her microphone, as though about to faint. "Death Row?! Death Rows are for redneck prisons, not feminist institutes of correctology!"

Feeling more secure of her place in The Big Chair, Ester intended to call a brief court recess, but..."Here's another one, here's another one, here's another raper," someone shouted. The twitchy female co-ed who had testified earlier jittered her way through the crowd and placed onto the platform..."Hide your self, hide your sister. Hide your self, hide your sister. He so dumb, he so dumb. He can't run off an' tell 'cause..." The bust of one of Ester's male predecessors, previously on display at a Rotunda entrance, had obviously triggered another painful "trombone" to the already bruised and fragile psyche of the youngish victim. With her blood risen, Ester too now felt she had been traumatized by sight of the bronze sculpture that had stood atop a phallic pedestal in a hallway.

"OFF WITH THE HEAD!"

THIRTY-ONE

Watching the frightful goings-on inside the OIC Rotunda—and jotting notes in a little spiral book—Henryetta felt like the young girl in *Alice and Wonderland* who went down a rabbit hole. Dean Frigg, yelling "Off with their heads!" every two minutes, reminded her of the movie's giant-headed Red Queen of course. Except in the Dean's case—with her wearing a red dress <u>and</u> plopped onto a red cushion in a big chair—it was her <u>hind</u> end that looked so unusually huge. Her settin' there with a microphone stand leaned between her legs, spread like a football player on a bench, also made for unsightly strangeness. Not that the Dean's head wasn't semi-scary too, what with her hair wild and hanging down; her face smeared with mascara and lipstick. And in a grim kind of Wonderland way, the nonsensical "trials"... Uh oh, now Ballsheviks had ahold of Coach Buster Downs by both of his arms, and were escortin' him through the mob toward the platform to face Dean Frigg and G.G. Carpenter.

Down with love muscles! Down with dongs! Down with schlongs! Down with...

The *Feminismo!* editor pointed a long finger at the coach. "You, sir, a faculty member of sorts, are hereby accused of committing a particularly heinous sexual assault on a defenseless victim, in public! What do you have to say for yourself?" Dean Frigg's head started to droop, like she was nodding off or somethin'.

Coach Buster, dressed in a tight semi-revealing rassler's outfit, adjusted a noticeable bulge in the area of his privates, and said, "Huh?"

"So you lust to inflict more pain on the defenseless victim, I see," said Ms. Carpenter. "Okay, I guarantee: You will pay, and pay dearly for subjecting her to the further humiliation of having to tell her sad story again, in public." She turned her head to the side and said: "Have the victim step forward. We don't want a pseudo faculty member whining to the Supreme Court about not being allowed to face his accuser."

Down with whangers! Down with whangers! Down with whangers! Down with...

A husky gal with blonde, braided pigtails, wearing a pink rasslin' outfit, stepped in front of the platform next to the OIC football coach.

"Ms. X, please tell the court in your own words what this man did to you last night after knocking you to the very floor you are now, miraculously, able to stand upon without medical assistance."

"Well," said the gal, looking at the coach in a friendly way, "he made a Hopping Bunny move and tried to get me into a Banana Split. I got out of that with a left-sided Slippery Nipple. But then I made the fatal mistake of trying a Fan move..."

Dean Frigg's head popped up. "Fan move?!" she said, lifting a cheek of her oversized bottom. "Which fan move?"

"Counter-clockwise," the gal answered, "which was when Coach got me in a Viennese Oyster position and pinned me with an Organ Grinder that I didn't have the muscle strength to fight off. I didn't know I had been raped 'til you told me," she said to "Gigi."

Down with organs! Down with organs! Down with organs! Down with...

"And I didn't know that particular one-two combination was illegal under the Unisex Wrestling Federation's new rules," Coach Downs said. "I used to do it lots of times against lots of gals a lot less muscular than Georgette."

Down with grinders! Down with grinders! Down with grinders! Down with...

"You sir, you hideous monster, should have your organ ground <u>off</u> with an electric sander!"

"Yes! Off with his flat-topped head!" said Dean Frigg. "Next case."

Coach Downs' victim, "Georgette," walked toward the prison exit, arm and arm with him, smilin' all the way to the door leading outside to an open gate in the walls. Henryetta semi-hoped "Sheep Dog Murphy" would get charged with sex assault, so she could get him out early too. The stench of mixed left-over odors—bacon, fried Rocky Mountain oysters and burned-up falsies—was about more than a body could tolerate. Not to mention the racket.

Down with woodies! Down with stiffies! Down with joysticks! Down with...

Ms. Carpenter leaned down and whispered into Dean Frigg's ear. "No, absolutely not; you go too far, Gigi," the Dean shouted. "That particular person is utterly incapable of sexual assault."

"The burden of proof is on the accused, Ester; even under your own wimpy rules."

"Not in this case. If you read the rule carefully, you will see that it does not apply when the accuser is male."

"Very well, have it your way, Ester. I shall take on the burden and prosecute the charge." Ms. Carpenter looked out into the crowd. "Have Mr. Buddy Brown brought forward."

Down with little buddies! Down with little buddies! Down with little buddies! Down with...

What in tarnation! Was Buddy gonna accuse Mr. Shat of assaulting Dean Frigg last night in the conjugatin' room? Or vica versa?

"Mr. Brown, tell this tribunal what you know about a certain participant in the rape epidemic that has put women on this campus into a state of terror."

"Well, I just hope I can help by doing the right thing," said Buddy, with a goody-goody smile at Dean Frigg. "I happened to run across some confidential conjugal visit records in a locked safe. I thought Dean Frigg should know who is doing what in that private room, so I put the info online; after blacking out the identity of the assault victim, of course."

"Tell us who went in there to do—what else but—commit rape."

"Leon Corn. He went in there about two and a half weeks ago...

Down with corn! Down with corn! Down with corn! Down with...

"...and tried to get me to go in there, with rubbers! I thought Dean Frigg should know, since Leon..."

"Is my crowning achievement in male behavior correction!" Dean Frigg thundered. "I can assure you, Gigi, Mr. Corn's sexual conduct has been entirely proper since I took charge three weeks ago."

"So-called 'moderate' means of male correction never work,

Ester."

"No, Gigi! I will not have you besmirch my prize specimen," said the Dean, standing. "I am writing a book and need him to remain here under my study. In fact..." She turned her face to the mob. "Bring Mr. Corn to the forefront. I want my 'esteemed' colleague to see firsthand what correct corrrectology can do to males."

Down with manhood! Down with manhood! Down with manhood!

Henryetta's heart went out to poor Leon, 'til he stepped up with such a big grin on his shaved face, looking so proud of hisself.

"Take down your trousers, Mr. Corn," Dean Frigg commanded, which he did without complaint.

Ha, ha, ha, ha, ha, ha, ha, ha, ha, ha, ha, ha...

"See, Gigi, my specimen's testicles, once the size and texture of coconuts, have been reduced to bleached prunes, without radical application of expensive radiation. I have personally squeezed every ounce of testosterone out of Mr. Corn. He is now a model correctee."

Ha, ha, ha, ha, ha, ha, ha, ha, ha, ha, ha, ha, ha, ha, ha, ha, ha...

Leon looked down at his privates and started mumbling, "This is my penis, it's not a gun. It's only for peeing, not for fun. This is my penis, it's not a gun..."

"Good for you, Ester. But as of two and a half weeks ago those coconuts were being used to bludgeon a helpless victim in a despicable room specifically designated for hetero-fornication on OIC premises under your nominal command!"

"There is no proof of that. His mother may have visited him there to confidentially deliver a sack of cookies."

"Indeed we <u>do</u> have proof, my dear Ester," said G.G. Carpenter, as a feminista pushed a cart and TV monitor to a side of the platform. "Roll the security tape!"

Uh oh, Henryetta had a feeling she her own self was gonna get embarrassed, but...There must have been a video tape mix-up, 'cause the picture that came onto the screen showed only the corridor leading from the Rotunda to... Uh oh again. Sure enough, there she was, noticeable as a carbuncle on a movie star's nose, pinning Buddy Brown to the corridor wall, then dragging him toward the conjugatin' room, but...The lights in the Rotunda flickered and the TV screen went blank.

"Did you see that?!" the Dean roared. "That little putz, Mr. Brown, copped a feel of that young defenseless woman's *derriere*, despite the fact she had clearly <u>not</u> made any pre-fondle fan move to affirmatively consent to such an assault!"

Down with little putzes! Down with little putzes! Down with little putzes! Down with...

Buddy sidled away from the platform, then applied his football running speed to..."Collar that little dormouse!" the Red Queen hollered. A gang of feministas tackled him before he could get back to his cell.

Down with little peckerwoods! Down with little peckerwoods! Down with little peckerwoods!

"Off with his head!"

Henryetta was relieved that poor Leon might not..."He be comin' up those stairs. He be snatchin' our peoples up. Hide your self, hide your sisters. Hide your self, hide your sisters. 'Cause he been rapin' everybody 'round here." It was that twitchy gal again—the one bruised and fragile from a sexual "trombone"—was yelling and pointing at Leon. "He so dumb, he so dumb. He don't have to confess 'cause..."

After another bunch of feministas had calmed her down some, the semi-regular assault victim told Dean Frigg she had been in a stairwell last night with someone named Antoine; had heard footsteps from below; had looked over a rail and seen Leon's shaved head rising up the stairs at her like the swollen tip of a giant pecker.

Then she fainted.

"This is my penis," said Leon in his defense, still looking down, "it's not a gun. It's only for peeing…"

Down with peters! Down with pee-pees! Down with fun guns! Down with…

"You have a crystal-clear choice, Ester," said G.G. Carpenter. "Either mete out severe punishment to this dangerous walking, talking Corn stalker of helpless women trapped in dark campus corners, or step down from your ODR position!"

"Okay, Gigi, you win," the Dean said, with a sigh. "Off with Mr. Corn's grotesquely bald head."

Henryetta, though some sorry to see Leon expelled from OIC—where he seemed to have got semi-corrected—also let out a sigh, in relief that she her own self had not got hauled into "court" for sex assaulting Buddy Brown in the OIC corridor.

THIRTY-TWO

Shat folded several sheets of toilet paper and put them in the pocket of his orange pants. Since dawn, he had penned a first chapter of a revised morality tale—**R***d Like Me**—from the female perspective of a "Shitner Poole." Now, for the last time, he looked around the concrete Death Row cell that had been his home for almost three weeks. But for the menace of Dean Frigg, he would not have minded serving a bit more of Sheep Dog Murphy's sentence. But no, he had previously learned the hard way not to stay too long at a party; and besides: Outside the walls, a party for two—Gigi and him—would be more zesty. She had sent four of her staff, all wearing rosy pink headbands matching hers, to serve as a kind of honor guard for his duck walk to freedom. Escorted into the corridor by her feministas, he saw that doors to all the Death Row cells were open; the concrete caves he sashayed past were all empty. Rabbit, Greasy, Big Tuna and his other bros seemed to have hooked up with Yellow Mama for a last hand; held onto those eights and aces; and bought the farm. So long suckers!

Dear old Harry's protege, Henryetta, spelled with a y, had

obviously dealt his own get-out-of-jail cards to Dean Frigg, Shat thought. His true identity had been restored. Such was his joy to again be Shatner Lapp—again a famous white journalist—he was inclined to think charitably of the Great Whore of Babylon, even before detecting the sound of a raucous farewell party for him in progress. Last night, sensing the weight of her school marm crush on him, so to speak, he had feared she might never release him. But now it seemed Ester Frigg was, after all, the proverbial Great Whore with a heart of gold. He'd had numerous send-offs through the years from various places of employment; surrounded by joyous bosses and colleagues, happy to see him move on with his career; but never one so...Holy smokin' doodads! There must have been three hundred women in the OIC Rotunda, all cheering his departure:

Down with penises! Down with pricks! Down with dongs! Down with...

Down with dicks ! Down with putzes! Down with schlongs! Down with...

Down with whangers! Down with weiners! Down with HIM! Down with HIM! Down with HIM! Down with......

A stage had been set up for speeches. Gigi, holding the shaft of an upright mic—and looking schweet!—stood on a stage, eagerly waiting to introduce him and..."Arghh!" Though traumatized to see Ester Frigg on the dais—draped in a bloody red cloak, sitting with legs apart in a large chair, cat hair dangling from her head in shreds—Shat put horrid images of last night's snarlin' encounter with her out of mind and mentally prepared appropriate remarks for the ceremony:

Almost four score days ago, I brought forth to this prison, a new idea. If I, once a baldfaced boy from Lancaster County, could dye my skin and bear the cross that Martin Luther King, Junior carried from

Selma by foot, could I not go forth from here by yellow Checker cab to hype the bad news about an R-word epidemic afoot at correctology institutes throughout the land? Here, at OIC, a naive, trusting young co-ed, Miss Shitner Poole, has penned a dramatic narrative of her own classicly traumatic experience on this campus. Fearful of not being believed, she has asked me to vouch for her, and so I shall, at some length. Shitner, who prefers to be called by her pet name, "Messy," came here, expecting to get drunk, get naked, and party-hearty in safe and secure men's fraternity cell blocks. But sad to say...

The cheering for him came to a halt, as he arrived in front of the stage.

"Before you waste our time with a hopeless plea for mercy," said Gigi, looking down upon him, "you might as well know that we have come into possession of confidential records proving that immediately upon your arrival at OIC, you sexually assaulted a young and defenseless woman in a 'love nest for couples' on campus premises."

"Identify that little tart at once!" the Great Whore roared. "Her pimp blotted out her name from the records. Who is she?"

Though startled by the rude inquisitorial tone of his farewell welcome, Shat readily admitted that he had briefly shared OIC's conjugal visiting room with a certain Henryetta Somebody. "We observed the Couples Only rule," he added, "and sent dear old Harry away. It wasn't a threesome."

"Write that down!" the frumious furry Frigger said, in reaction to which Shat, beginning to feel slightly nervous, reached into his pocket for a pen and...out spilled his toilet paper manuscript onto the floor. "Demoana, seize the evidence," the demon Dean then said, whereupon a vaguely familiar, roundish black gal hurried from beside the stage, scooped up the revised first chapter of **R***d Like Me**, and handed it to the bull dyke from hell. "Hmmm," she said, scanning the first page. Then: "What we have here is the little tart's written accusation against…" She looked down at him and belched. "My dear Mr. Murphy, please tell me: Are you or are you not the 'Great Hog of Babylon' whom Miss Poole claims assaulted her?"

"Give that to me!" Gigi shouted, crossing the stage, then snatching the toilet paper. "Aha!" she said. "So a Miss Shitner Poole is the true identity of 'Sheep Dog'. She's _my_ victim for _my_ big story! What have you done with her, 'Mr. Murphy'?"

"For your information, Gigi, Mr. Murphy is 'Sheep Dog'; it says so on his transfer papers from New Hampshire. What the court wants to know: Is that little tart, Miss Poole a/k/a Henryetta Somebody, in attendance?" The Great Whore pushed herself up in her chair, raised her head, and looked out upon the sea of assembled women like a hungry walrus sniffing for a scent of herring. "You can't hide," she bellowed. "I will hunt you down. I will find you. And you will be severely punished if you do not disavow your false charge of the R-word against Mr. Murphy."

"My Goddess, Ester!" said Gigi. "There is no such thing as a false charge of the R-word on campus, nor any such thing as an innocent man anywhere. And you call yourself a feminist!"

"Here I am," said a familiar voice from behind Shat. "I'm Henryetta Somebody." Thank God, he would be rescued from this madness, Shat thought, as Henryetta Somebody stepped to his side. "And this here is not really Sheep Dog Murphy," the feisty girl said; "this is Mr. Shatner Lapp, the famous newspaper reporter, who is not really black. It's just skin colortration."

"Yes, I teach that in my Sensitivity Training class," the walrus said. "While correct, as a rule, in this case the correct rule is beside the point. The correctness required of you, Miss

Poole, pertains to the as yet uncorrected record of your previously alleged relationship with Mr. Murphy, whom you now admit you mistook for your tormentor, a great hog named 'Mr. Lapp'."

"For crying out loud, Ester, I know this man disguised in blackface," Gigi finally acknowledged, to Shat's relief. "His name is Shatner Lapp. He is an incorrigible womanizer who routinely uses patriarchal authority to assault junior co-workers twice a day, on workplace desktops, in office building elevators, and at least once during the funeral service for a victim's mother. He is a beast!"

"His name is Jamus Murphy!" the frigging head of the OIC Title IX ODR insisted. "I know him quite well, Gigi, intimately in fact. He is not the sort of man who would lay a hand on a common tart, such as Miss Poole."

"He didn't lay on a hand," Henryetta confirmed. "He gave me some rubbers and told me to ride Leon Corn's leg."

"There you have it, Gigi. There is no evidence whatsoever that Mr. Murphy has ever sexually misbehaved; and I will not allow you to turn my OIC Title IX Office of Dispute Resolution into a kangaroo court!"

As one of Gigi's aides rushed to the stage and began to whisper in her ear, Shat resisted an urge to hug his savior, Henryetta Somebody, for fear the jealous walrus would lunge…"Aha!" Gigi cried out, before announcing that OIC security video records had been sorted out and re-spooled. "We shall she whether or not Miss Poole's written accusation is true. Roll the tape!"

On the screen of a TV set beside him…"Arghhh!" At the sight of the Great Whore standing astride him, lifting her skirt; revealing her humongous buttocks, with obvious intent to make a Flying Gamahooch move on him, Shat barfed onto his shoes.

"I was incapacitated by spiked punch!" the Great Whore

bellowed. "Me too!" shouted that double-doucing bitch, Gigi Carpenter. "We were rendered incapable of affirmative consent to this beastly assault!" they cried, as though singing from a shared hymnal.

Women's vaginas matter! Women's vaginas matter! Women's vaginas matter!

Though hurt by Gigi's disavowal of her part in the attempted three-way hobblin', gobblin', snarlin' shown on the TV screen, Shat's gratification that the two feminists had been hoisted on his own petard, so to speak, was schweet! Ironically, their rigged system for gender dispute resolution had worked, but against them.

"Off with his head!" Henryetta Somebody nevertheless shouted. "Let Mr. Shat go on about his business of writing down morality tales in newspapers and books."

"A clear case of R-word in reverse," said Dean Frigg, seeming to accept her defeat. "Crystal clear," Gigi agreed, but then... "He spiked our punch and led us to do things to him we cannot even remember," they sang, in perfect feminist harmony.

"Off with his head, dang it! Let him out of here!"

"Guilty! as approximately charged in the first degree," said Gigi. "No! Sentence first, verdict afterward!" roared the Great Walrus. "Guards! Take this man, whomever he may be, back to his cell."

"No, please, no," Shat pleaded, as a gang of feministas took hold of him more roughly than necessary. "I am not the man I used to be. I'm on your side now. I myself am a victim of the campus R-word epidemic. I am not Shatner Lapp, the famous journalist. I am not the oppressed African-American butcher, Sheep Dog Murphy. Can't you see beneath this wig and Oil of Shinola: I am Shitner Poole!"

But they wouldn't listen.

THIRTY-THREE

Outside the walls of OIC, Henryetta sat at the wheel of her parked yellow Checker—on the bias due to lack of tires on the right side—and fretted about the fate of Mr. Shat. It was almost sundown; nine or ten hours had passed since a gang of Ballsheviks had hauled him back to his cell. Dean Frigg had throwed his get-out-of-jail cards into the air like they had no more meaning than a deck of kings and queens and jacks. She didn't care what Mr. Shat's true identity was, nor about anything bad or good he might've done outside of prison. He had gave her the mitten—an old-fashioned term used by Henryetta's mother, Wynona Sue, for getting rejected by the one wanted—and for that offense, the Dean wasn't about to let Mr. Shat go unless legally forced to. That was worrisome, 'cause that Title IX seemed to have turned law inside OIC over to her.

On TV the Governor had said he couldn't do nothin' about the feminist revolution staged by Dean Frigg and Ms. Carpenter for fear of getting hauled into OIC's kangaroo court his own self on charges of sexually traumatizing two hundred female inmates under Title IX, "that gives those badass wenches federal

rights to more TLC than what's needed for hothouse orchids."
On the other hand, Mr. Harold was hopeful that his old friend,
Judge Swinford, back in Okmulgee County, would have enough
sand-in-the-sack to stand up to the Dean, but…Praise the Lord,
the truck her boss drove to and from his so-called "gentleman's
farm" pulled up next to her Checker and…Land sakes alive!
When he got out of the heavy-duty pick-up, she saw that mild-
mannered Mr. Harold was wearing a Smoky Bear hat and
carrying a double-barrel shotgun. "Don't worry, Henryetta," he
said when they got face-to-face in the OIC visitors parking lot,
"it's not loaded. But Judge Bill made me an honorary deputy
sheriff, which also entitles me to wear this here hat. And, oh
yeah, I've got his *habeas corpus* order—that's Latin for 'show me
the body'—right here in my pocket."

Body?

Her over-educated boss explained that the foreign language
term was just Judge Swinford's way of saying Dean Frigg had to
bring Mr. Shat to court, alive, so he could look the prisoner in
the eye and hear for himself what he had to say. "'Hell has no
fury like that of a spited woman'," Mr. Harold then said, holding
tight to the strap of his Smoky Bear hat as they headed into
fierce wind toward the visitors entrance to the prison. "But if I
know Shat, he'll be kissin' and huggin' on Dean Frigg to beat
the band. He'll cool her off by heatin' her up, if you know what
I mean."

At the check-in counter, one of those short-haired Ballshevik
feministas with a rosy pink headband running across her
forehead—but wearing a loose-fitting white dress—greeted
them with a bright smile, friendly as a Campfire Girl selling
cookies. "I'm sorry, but Dean Frigg is making rounds and leading
evensong at the moment," she said, "but if you would care to

have a seat…May I serve you cookies and a nice cup of tea?" Mr. Harold declined the offered hospitality, and showed the court order. "Go down that corridor, cross the Rotunda and use the exit marked 'Cell Block D'," the new OIC greeter said, pointing a finger. "But please note: Co-Deans Frigg and Carpenter allow no phallic means of traumatizing women on campus, so you will have to leave your shotgun with me. And your hat."

Evensong?

"End of the day choral prayers," Mr. Harold explained, and as they neared the Rotunda, Henryetta heard the singing of women's voices, though the words didn't sound like prayers to her. *If we catch an A.D. Bull inside these college walls/ We'll take him to the Rec Hall and amputate his balls.* The smoke and odor from earlier had cleared out, and when they got to the Rotunda, she saw that all the cell doors seemed to be open. Women inmates, all in flowing white dresses, stood on the overhead tiers of walkways, singing: *If a Jewish Jihadi yells for mercy, this is what we'll do/ We'll stuff his ass with broken glass, and seal it up with glue.* Passing through the doorway to Cell Block D, followed by waning sounds of evensong, a sign with an arrow painted on it said they were headed for Death Row. *The women of OIC/ They fight for their chastity/ Fight everyone but we/ The women of OIC.*

Henryetta felt a little shiver when lights blinked off and on, and the singing behind them faded out. Engineers were still testing Mama Megawatt, she reckoned, as they reached an also blinking overhead neon sign: *Welcome to DEATH ROW/ Abandon All Hope Ye Who Enter Here.* Both Mr. Harold and her stopped dead-still outside the open entry to the row and peeked inside. All the cell doors in there seemed to also be opened and…Land sakes alive! G.G. Carpenter stepped out of one of the cells and started in their direction. She had got herself cleaned up; redressed in a clean white pantsuit as well as a fresher-looking headband; and carried a wad of tangled hair in her hand.

Soon as the *Femichismo!* editor got to where they stood, Mr. Harold held up the "show me the body" order and stated their business. "Ester is with Shat down the hallway," she said. "We had a few drinks at our Co-Deans' house across the road and came over here to torment him with evensong. Shat began to hit on her. Ester, playing coy, assumed a face down—utterly obscene—stretching-cat pose on his concrete bed; and spotted this." Ms. Carpenter held out the wad of hair. "It was wedged into a crack at the foot of Shat's concrete 'Cadillac'. The poor, dear 'cat person' thinks it's what's left of Martha Washington, and no doubt it is. Ester had 'Martha's' shed fur weaved into hairdo extensions for herself, to fill-out the buns she wears on her head. I suspect she lost an extension in Shat's dorm room during a prior 'visit', but...Poor thing is distraught. Prior to publication in *Femichismo!* I should say nothing more about her conniption fit, nor anything about her vengeful fury, but off the record..."

From somewhere came the sound of evensong, in solo:

Do your balls hang low? Do they swing to and fro?/ Can you tie 'em in a knot? Can you tie 'em in a bow?

Can you throw 'em o'er your shoulder, like a macho-man soldier?/ Can you do the double shuffle when your balls hang low?

Would it make 'em wanna dance, if I took down your pants?/ Would it make you feel brave, if they got a close shave?

Would they make a pretty pair, if I strapped 'em in a chair?/ Can you do the Dutch shuffle when your balls hang low?

The lights went off...

...and stayed off...

...for at least three minutes...

...and then some...

"Mr. Shat! It's Henryetta Somebody. Are you okay in there?"
The overhead neon sign began to blink.
Then all the lights came back to life.
"What in tarnation!"
Dean Frigg staggered down the aisle between Death Row cells, taking off large, padded, rubber gloves as she approached, one of which looked semi-singed around its edges. With a bare hand, she reached into a pocket of her red pantsuit and…Great balls afire! The Dean commenced to blow her nose into what looked like the frizzy jet black wig that had been sewed onto Mr. Shat's scalp! From behind her, a cloud of smoke came rolling through Death Row from an opened doorway at the other end, bringing with it an odor—not of fried bacon—more like the semi-sweet aroma of roasted Rocky Mountain oysters.

THE END

BACKWORD

The Walrus and the Carpenter
Walked on a mile or so.
And then they rested on a rock
Conveniently low:
And all the little Oysters stood
And waited in a row.

'A loaf of bread,' the Walrus said,
'Is what we chiefly need;
Pepper and vinegar besides
Are very good indeed -
Now if you're ready, Oysters dear,
We can begin to feed.

'It was so nice of you to come!
And you are so very nice!'
The Carpenter said nothing but
'Cut us another slice:
I wish you were not so deaf -
I've had to ask you twice!'

'It seems a shame,' the Walrus said,
'To play them such a trick,
After we've brought them out so far,
And made them trot so quick!'
The Carpenter said nothing but
'The butter's spread too thick!'

'I weep for you,' the Walrus said:
'I deeply sympathize.'
With sobs and tears he sorted out
Those of the largest size,
Holding a pocket handkerchief
Before his streaming eyes.

'O Oysters,' said the Carpenter,
'You've had a pleasant run!
Shall we be trotting home again?'
But answer came there none -
And this was scarcely odd because
They'd eaten every one.

Abridged, from Alice's Adventures in Wonderland by Lewis Carroll.

Made in the USA
Charleston, SC
06 April 2015